I0543211

IMPASSABLE FORCE

FORCE OF NATURE SERIES

BOOK 8

By

KATHI S. BARTON

World Castle Publishing, LLC

This is a work of fiction. Names, characters, places, and incidents are products of the author's imagination or are used fictitiously and are not to be construed as real. Any resemblance to actual events, locations, organizations, or person, living or dead, is entirely coincidental.

WCP

World Castle Publishing, LLC
Pensacola, Florida

Copyright © Kathi S. Barton 2014
ISBN: 9781629890685
First Edition World Castle Publishing, LLC, March 7, 2014
http://www.worldcastlepublishing.com

Licensing Notes

All rights reserved. No part of this book may be used or reproduced in any manner whatsoever without written permission, except in the case of brief quotations embodied in articles and reviews.

Cover: Karen Fuller
Editor: Eric Johnston

CHAPTER 1

"I've made arrangements to leave him," Mary said. Molly looked at her sister as she continued. "I've found a lawyer that seems to know his shit and has sworn to me that Carter will never know what hit him until it's too late. I have to do this now. I'm sick to death of having to lie about the bruises and his inability to be nice to me."

Molly looked out over the yard she and Mary had been walking in. It wasn't all that far from the house really, but there were no cameras here and no way for Carter to walk in on them while they were talking. Molly hated her brother-in-law almost as much as Mary did. But Mary had tried this before and had ended up in the hospital for a month when he'd found out. Molly knew her sister needed this and if this guy fucked her over, Molly would rip his ass up.

"I want you to do this. You have to. But what does he get out of this? Divorce? Will you have to pay him anything to support him?" Mary shook her head. "I don't believe it. He'll have some slick lawyer take you to the cleaners and when he does that, what will you do then?"

"Start over. You know that none of this means as much to me as it ever did to him. I only have this house because he wanted it and back then, I wanted him to be happy." Mary looked over the fields toward the house. "For all I care he can have it all. I've got what I wanted. Doing what I do is fun for me, not so much like a job. Carter was...he was something...Carter was a mistake. A huge one. And now I can see that he only stayed with me this long for the money."

Molly knew he'd been the wrong person for her sister long before they were married. She'd even gone so far as to tell her sister that he was only after her money. But Mary had told her she was in love. It had taken her being put in the hospital for Molly to find out the real truth. She'd married the bastard thinking he was saving her. Molly would never forgive Carter for that. She looked at Molly when she spoke again.

"Those cameras that you put in for me worked well when I went to see the lawyer. He was able to get a clear picture of Carter doing what he does best. My lawyer is a nice guy, his name is Phil Campbell. You'd like him. There's something about him that...I know it sounds weird, but I didn't think he was normal." Mary shook her head as she continued. "Anyway. The camera in our bedroom. He asked me if I had proof that Carter was seeing anyone, and I pulled out my tablet. I'm so glad you showed me how to look in on the house while away. When I showed him the one in our bedroom, Carter was fucking someone. Well, he was doing more than that, but you get the idea."

"What did the lawyer say?" Molly wasn't going to trust anyone just yet. She'd had to look into several other lawyers for her sister and all of them had some connection to Carter. Even if it had been someone he'd had a drink with or even walked by at the club, he was off the list of anyone she wanted her sister to use. Molly was going to protect her sister at all costs.

"He thought it was a recording. I assured him that it was not." Mary laughed, something Molly hadn't heard her do in a long time. "I had to show him that the camera was set up with the timestamp on it. He was impressed with your work as well as pissed that Carter could be so callous."

"Carter needs to be ended." Mary didn't say anything and Molly didn't either. Sometimes, Molly knew that her sister needed to do things her own way rather than be bullied. And Molly knew that she was a great bullier.

They turned to head back when the force of something hit her so hard it pitched her forward. Pain cascaded all over her body like she'd been drenched in it. As she fell forward into the grass, she saw her sister fall too. Molly heard the report of the gunshot echo over the hillside just as she was shot again. This time the pain was sickening and she knew that someone was trying to kill them. Pain made her sick, and she threw up twice before moving to her sister. But something warm, blood likely, was blurring her vision.

"Molly?" Molly made herself move to her sister when she said her name. At first she couldn't see her, but when she did, she had to sit up a little to make sure it was her. There was so much blood that Molly was sure she'd had it dumped on her. But a third shot rang out and Molly laid back down.

"Don't move. I don't know where the shots are coming from, so just lay still." Mary didn't answer her, and Molly was afraid. "Mary, please answer me."

"He's doing this. Carter. He's trying to kill me." Molly didn't answer her because her mind was racing to figure out how to get them out of this. She reached for her cell phone just as another shot hit her in the leg.

Molly was going to kill the bastard if she lived through this. He'd fucking shot them. When the operator answered the phone, Molly gave her everything she would need to send out the troops.

"This is Sergeant Molly Barker, badge number nine-three-seven." She gave her the address where she was and where they were in the yard. "I need an ambulance as well as support. There is a sniper shooting at us."

"The team in on the way." Molly closed her eyes. The pain was making her dizzy again, and she knew that she was losing blood too fast to survive. "Do you know who the shooter is?"

"No." She didn't and wouldn't say so even if she knew it was Carter. He was hers, and she was fucking going to take him out even if she lost her badge because of it. The dispatcher asked her several more questions, none of which Molly could answer. She looked over at Mary again and saw that her eyes were closed.

"Mary?" No answer, and Molly felt her heart pound. Moving slowly, she reached over and nearly cried out when she felt her sister's pulse. It was slow but help was on the way. She started talking because she wanted her sister to live, and she had to do something. When talking to Mary and getting no answers again scared her, she started talking to the dispatcher.

"The shots have stopped for now. There were five total. All coming from the West." Molly turned slightly to see the house. "The house is south of where we are. My sister, Mary Ravenhall, is with me."

"The ETA for the squad and ambulance is about three minutes." Molly nodded and felt the phone slip from her fingers. She was losing blood fast, she knew, and could no longer feel her legs. The shakes started almost as soon as she could hear the sirens. They'd save Mary.

Someone was talking to her. When Molly opened her eyes, she looked at the blurry man in front of her and pulled her gun up to shoot him. Someone pressed her hand back to the ground, and he laughed.

"Good guy here. If you promise to let go of the gun, I'll finish patching you up." Molly tried twice to tell him to forget her and go to Mary, but he seemed to understand. "She's been loaded up already and on her way to life flight. She is in bad shape."

"Shoot." He nodded, and she felt her gun being pulled from her fingers. "I need that back in case they come back."

"You don't have to worry, I've got it." She glanced at the other man standing over her and had to close her eyes. She couldn't have made him out if her life depended on it. "It's your captain. What the fuck are you doing out here getting shot to shit?"

"I was bored to death and thought I'd pissed someone off. You know how I am." He laughed, and she closed her eyes again against the pain. "Mary is hurting. Can you make sure she gets the best? And someone outside her door?"

"I'm going to watch over the two of you. I'll keep you both safe. My favorite actress is in that chopper and my...well, my best investigator is laying here shot to shit." Captain Martin Huffman would, too. He was like a bear with his cubs when someone from his department was hurt in the line of duty. "You want to tell me what you know?"

"No." He said he didn't think she would. "Hurt." She was, too. Her entire body felt as if she'd been shot several times and was bleeding out. Molly smiled a little, knowing that was just what had happened. When someone lifted her up, she couldn't have stopped the scream if someone had put a gun to her head. She was moving down the road when she thought of something.

"My sister. She had allergies to some meds." The man with her said he knew, that it had been on her paperwork when they'd called it in. "I'm not going to make it, am I?"

The medic looked at her for a long while before he shrugged. "You've been shot four times. The one in your chest is bleeding so bad that I think whoever hit you hit something vital. And the one in your leg grazed your artery there, too. You're bleeding faster than we can put it in you."

"My sister. Will you tell her that I'm sorry?" He nodded. "Tell her…tell her to run and hide." Her body started to get cold, and she felt the tears run down her face. Breathing became harder, and she could feel herself slipping away. Death was coming, and there wasn't a fucking thing she could do about it.

Molly closed her eyes as she started to fade out. Memories, most of them with Mary, swirled around in her head so quickly that she was sick from the motion. But as they started to fade as well, she felt as if she was being given a great gift in seeing her sister once more before she died. Molly let death take her.

~~~

Phil woke with a start. He had no idea what had disturbed his rest, but he knew that whatever it was, it was huge. As soon as he reached for Holly, he knew that someone was coming toward the two of them. He started to let his beast go but realized at the last minute that it was Randy Atkins. The man was on a mission.

As soon as he knocked on the door, Phil got up and moved toward it. When he knocked a second, then a third time, Phil decided that the man had to learn some manners in a vampire's house. But as soon as he looked at the younger man, he knew that whatever had happened was worth what he was doing.

"What is it? Is it the family? What happened?" He felt Holly rise as well and moved into the hall. Randy was shaking, he was so upset. "Take a deep breath and let it out slowly."

"The actress, the one that was here the other day? She's been shot." Phil thought of the video that he'd seen of the husband and knew that he'd shot his wife. "They're taking her to surgery now. She and another woman were shot several times when they were out walking the estate. If he finds out about the divorce, he might pay someone to finish the job. I've already sent a bunch of the pack over to keep an eye on them. My friend at the hospital said they're both in bad shape. The younger one coded twice on the way to the hospital."

"When did this happen?" Phil moved toward the stairs, agreeing with Randy. The man would lose a great deal when the divorce went through. And a good deal more if she died and he was guilty of the crime. He went to his office as he willed clothes on his body. The robe would not do if he had to leave soon.

"About an hour ago. Like I said, I have a friend on the force, and he called me about ten minutes ago. I had someone watching for reports of abuse, and when her name came up, he called." Phil knew that Randy was going to make a good lawyer. Hell, the boy knew more people than he did, and it seemed that all of them owed him a favor. He answered the phone on the first ring, then looked at him as he relayed the information. "The other woman is her sister. A Molly Barker. She's on the police force in that area. They said she isn't expected to make it."

Mary had talked about her sister as much as she had her cheating husband. She was the one that had convinced her sister to file for divorce. She had also been the one that had taught Miss Ravenhall how to fight in all those action scenes that were in her movies. Phil had watched several of them after she'd left his office and was more impressed with the young actress.

They were headed to the hospital when Phil's phone rang. It was the hospital. Apparently Miss Ravenhall had told someone to contact him. He told the operator that he was on his way.

"If you can get here sooner rather than later, it'd be better. Both of the women are in bad shape." Phil told Holly to go faster and assured the woman on the phone he would be there soon. "She's been asking for you. And her sister. We've not told her yet how extensive the injuries were to her. But I think Miss Ravenhall knows. Phil...I don't think either of them are going to last the hour."

Phil was standing near the door going into intensive care just as a man came down the hall. He was the husband. It wasn't hard to tell that he had been with another woman when this had happened, but Phil would bet his last dollar that he had been a part of it. When he was near him, Carter Ravenhall looked him over like he was a bug on a wall.

"What the fuck do you think you're doing here? My wife didn't call you in." Phil didn't answer but continued to stare at him. "I asked you a question, you little bastard.

What the fuck do you think you're doing here with my wife?"

"You know, I almost didn't recognize you with your clothes on. You're the husband, aren't you?" Carter sneered at him. "Yes, I remember you now. Wife beater and cheater. Did you really think you'd get away with this?"

"You think you know so much? Well, I got news for you. She's fucking terrified of me and if she hired you to keep tabs on me, then you should also know that you'll be better off letting me buy whatever you think you have. I won't allow her to divorce me." Phil only looked at Randy as he came toward them. The young man looked like he'd take on Carter without breaking a sweat.

"Oh, I'm not an investigator. I'm a lawyer." Phil smiled when Carter took a step back. "And she has divorced you. I filed the paperwork myself. You should have been notified when it happened. I'm thinking you might have been lost in the works. Miss Ravenhall is no longer married to you. I'll have copies of it sent to you when I think about it. Or not. I'm not sure what I'll do concerning you."

"No. You can't have done that, I know. Someone would have told me. You were supposed to tell me." Phil shook his head. "There is no way she can divorce me without me knowing it. I put a stop to all the other times, and you can't do it without me knowing it. You're full of shit."

"So you said. Several times as a matter of fact. But, alas, I don't play by your rules." When Carter drew back to hit him, Phil started to stop him, but Randy held his hand over his head until he looked like he was going to break it. "Don't hurt the idiot. If you do, I might have to hurt him more just to be even."

Randy laughed and let Carter go. Even as old as he was with special powers as a vampire, Phil would not fuck with Randy Atkins. He was impassable when he wanted to be. Before he could say anything else, like Phil cared what it might be, the doctor came toward them. He didn't look like a man who was carrying good news.

"She won't settle until she talks to you." Phil nodded and took the green robe and slippers that he was handed. "Her sister is still in surgery and will...well, I'd like for you to settle her down. So do whatever you can to do that. Lie if you have to."

"He's not going in there without me." Carter started to shove his body forward, no doubt used to this sort of tactic working for him in the past. But Randy moved him back with a small shove. Phil wasn't sure, but he thought Randy had let a little of his beast go as well. Carter moved back to the wall and didn't say a word while Phil entered the small recovery room. The smell of death and blood nearly overwhelmed him.

"Miss Ravenhall?" When she didn't answer, he moved closer to the bed. He could see that she was attached to several machines and one of them showed her heart rate. It wasn't good. He said her name a little louder, and she looked at him.

"Molly? Is she dead?" He shook his head, not sure what he was supposed to do when he couldn't lie to her. "She's my savior. I told you that before."

"You did. I filed the paperwork and did just what I told you I would. Everything is in order." She closed her eyes and smiled. Phil watched her until she opened them again.

"She will be so mad at me." Phil thought that was an understatement but said nothing. "I should have listened to her sooner and left him. But I wanted it to work out. No, that's not true. I didn't want the press to find out that I'd failed."

"It's doubtful that your fans would think you could fail at anything." She laughed slightly, and the monitors started beeping. "Miss Ravenhall, is there anything else I can do for you?"

Phil knew that she was as good as dead. There was no way she'd be able to come back from the damage done to her. He was surprised that she was this coherent. The wrapping around her head did nothing to hide the fact that she'd been shot twice in the head. He could tell there was damage done to her brain.

"I wanted you to do one more thing for me." He nodded and waited while she seemed to fade out before she spoke again. It was hard to hear her even with his excellent hearing. "Make Molly understand that what I've done for her is what was necessary. She never would take anything from me. I want her to...."

When she faded out this time, the monitors showed that her heart had stopped. Two nurses came into the room, but before they could shove him away, her heart started beating again. He moved closer to her when the nurse told him she wanted him.

"I'm dead, we both know that." Phil nodded. "Tell Molly that she has to live for me. I know that sounds like a line from one of my movies, but she must do it for me. Find a good man and have babies for me."

"She might not make it." He couldn't lie to her. He wouldn't. The woman wanted more than he might be able to give her. "Your sister is in bad shape, too."

Mary smiled at him, and he felt his heart burst with love for her strength. "She'll live. She's much too strong and stubborn not to, but how she lives will be what matters. Tell her to live. Not just breathe."

This time when the monitors went off, Phil knew that she was gone. He stood nearby in the event that she did wake again, but the doctor that had come in at some point called her death. Mary Ravenhall was dead.

Phil moved out of the room. Randy was standing against the wall across from him, and all he did was shake his head. He would understand. Phil stood there trying to get his mind to wrap around that his client was dead and that he'd fallen in love with her a little in the short time he'd known her.

"She wasn't just a client, you know." Randy nodded. "I know that she was only in the office three times, but I swear to you it was as if I'd known her my entire life."

"Because of some bastard who liked to use her as a punching bag." Randy moved away from the wall just as Phil noticed Carter coming toward him. He started to warn Randy to behave, but right now he'd like to take a swing at the man, too. But all Randy did was stand in front of him. It was all it took to have the larger man hit at Randy.

Pressing charges was great. Randy had a bloodied lip to show the police, and Phil and the rest of the staff told them that Randy had been only standing there when the man had hit him. He was being taken away when Phil realized that he'd not been told his wife was gone.

"He doesn't deserve to know just yet." Phil agreed with the doctor. "I've filled out the paperwork with the police. And I've given them all the other reports I've had on Miss Ravenhall."

Phil thanked him and went down the hall to the waiting room. He wanted to be there in the event Molly Barker needed him. She would live even if he had to convert her to make sure she did.

CHAPTER 2

Randy watched the man who more than likely killed his wife. He sat in the chair across from him and Phil as if he were the king of the world and he was going to get by with everything. Little did he know that Jodie, Randy's sister-in-law, who sat at the table with them, was reading his every thought and sending that information to Phil. Randy simply watched.

"You think you can run this through without me saying a word is stupid." Phil said nothing to the man. "As soon as my lawyer gets here, I'm going to be the richest man in the world. And have the sympathy of the entire world at my beck and call."

Randy looked at Jodie when she laughed. She winked at him and then leaned back in the chair as she spoke. "Your lawyer? I'm thinking that you should make another few calls first. The estate lawyer is sitting across from you, and, believe it or not, I don't think he's on your side. The one you had coming is being...detained, I guess I'd say."

"Who the fuck are you?" Randy stood up when Carter did. "Oh, sit your ass down, boy. When I want something to eat or drink, I'll have you go and fetch it for me. What the hell is going on around here?"

"As I have told you twice now, you're here so that the will can be read. I can't do that without a witness from your side of the table. Your ex-wife was very clear on that part."

"She was not my ex-wife. We were still married when she died, and I'll have you know that whatever you think you have there isn't going to stand up in court because I have a good deal more experience with bitches than you do." Randy had to cover his mouth to hide the fact that he was laughing...and hard. If anyone at this table knew anything about bitches, that would be Phil. He was married to one. And Holly Campbell was only a good bitch when it suited her.

"Your lawyer is here." Jodie stood up when a man entered the room. She turned to look at him, and Randy did as well. Whatever had happened to slow him down was showing on his clothes. He looked as if he'd been dipped in mud and if his smell was any indications, some shit as well. By the time he came around the table, even Randy could tell that Carter was pissed off.

"What the fuck took you so long? I told you to be here at ten. It's nearly eleven-thirty now." The other man didn't answer but sat down. They'd have to get rid of the chair when he left, Randy knew it.

"I'm here now, so let's get this finished." The man looked at Phil before he continued. "I spent the better part of yesterday after the funeral looking for something to indicate that the paperwork you sent me wasn't legal. But everything seems to be in order. I'm impressed."

"Thank you." Phil handed a file full of papers to Carter and his lawyer as Jodie got up to leave. She was nearly to the door when Phil stopped her. "There anything else I need to know?"

"Nope. He's given it all up." She looked at him. "This was a great idea. Thanks for letting me be a part of it."

He'd told Phil that having information would likely save the other woman's life. She was barely hanging on as it was, and the guard outside the door to her room had seen to it that she lived longer. Three men had approached the room since she'd been moved to it, and he thought if they could find out how far Carter would go to have her killed, then they might be able to make sure that Miss Ravenhall's last wish was carried out. And they might be lucky enough to hang the man while they were at it.

"As you can see, Miss Ravenhall filed for divorce over eight months ago. The paperwork had been lost in the courthouse filing system until three months ago. At that time, I filed another paper showing just cause to have this divorce finalized so that—"

"What the fuck are you talking about? You can't have anything finalized without my say. You tell them that." Carter looked at the lawyer and then at Phil. "You're a liar. There is no way she'd take the…there is no way."

"Be that as it may, she had filed for divorce and was granted it by a judge three months ago." Randy didn't take his eyes off Carter. The man was ready to blow.

It was all a fabrication. In the past week, just after Mary had come to their office, he and Phil had been working around the clock to make things final for the woman. It had taken some fancy mind work on his brother's part and a good deal of help from some of the wolves that answered to Austin to get things in the correct order. The first divorce papers had been delayed by Carter. He had a man on the inside as well, but Phil had been a good deal stronger and had a lot of magic. Randy thought it was brilliant.

"I want a second opinion." Everyone stared at Carter as he stood up. Randy was ready for him to try anything, but he seemed to have more control over himself than they thought. He supposed the night in jail had done wonders for that.

"You can have all the opinions you want, but right now the locks are being changed on the house, the car you have driven here has been taken, and your credit cards have been canceled." Phil looked at him. "Did I miss anything?"

"Someone will be taking the jewelry he has on. Remember, it's a part of the estate now." Phil nodded and looked at Carter as Randy ran down his list of things he was supposed to take care of. "You'll also be banned from the county club as well as anything else that Miss Ravenhall owned. This includes any and all rights to her movies and any deals she was working on. She didn't put your name on any of that. Smart girl. Speaking of which, you'll also no longer be welcomed on the lots where she was filming. You'll find that the money you had stashed overseas is no longer there either. We took care of that yesterday."

"You can't do that." Phil pointed out that they could and they did. "Well, I want it all back. She was my wife, and as such, I'm taking all of her money as well as all that property she owned. We owned it together."

"Actually, you didn't. Own it together, I mean. She never put your name on anything she had prior to your marriage and since. Like I said, she was a smart girl. I wonder if her lovely sister had anything to do with that? She was a smart woman, too, if you ask me." Randy stood when Carter did. "Do it. I know you want to, so come on and try to knock me down. You'll be picking your ass up for months."

"I want what's coming to me." His spittle ran down his chin as he glared at him from across the table. Randy was not backing down either. The man had killed his wife and tried to murder her sister. And if what Jodie and Reid had figured out was true, this wasn't the first time he'd done something like this.

"Oh, I'm sure you'll get what's coming to you. In due time." Randy picked up his briefcase when Phil did. The other lawyer looked like he was relieved to have this over with. Randy didn't really blame him. Randy had known that Carter's first choice for a lawyer had dropped him right after talking to Phil. The man didn't think he wanted to go up against him. Randy was learning that Phil was not only a good lawyer but a respected one as well. Randy hoped that he'd be half the man he was when he was out on his own. They were back in the limo going to the office when Phil turned to him.

"I've been thinking. I'd like to have you as a full partner." Randy was shocked. When he'd first come to work with Phil, he'd told him several times that it was just a place for him to get his feet wet, and Randy had been fine with that. "You could go in halves with me and we'd branch out a bit. I know that you've a good many contacts, most of which I envy. But I think we'd make a good team."

"I'm...I don't know what to say." Phil nodded and handed him a file. "You've already drawn up the contracts?"

"Pretty much. I was going to wait and ask you next week when you finished with that trial, but I couldn't wait. I want to get this going." Randy knew that whatever was in the contact between them would benefit him more than Phil. The man had been around for a very long time and had everything he needed. And his daughter and mate were what he treasured most of all.

"I don't...are you sure about this? What if I lose?" He was afraid that he was going to. He'd gone into this trial with the thoughts of winning. Now he wasn't so sure. Things had taken a wrong turn yesterday.

"I have no doubt you'll pull it off. Besides, as you've said to me many times, you're going to live your life as a lawyer, and nothing nor anyone was getting in the way. I'm betting that win or lose at this trial, you'll still be a better man than most." Randy flushed. He didn't do well with compliments and looked away as Phil continued. "Look it over, and if you want to change anything, let me know. I think we can work out anything you want."

"I'm moving away." Phil nodded when he turned to look at him. "I know that family is everything, so please don't preach that to me again. But they're all so...."

"Happy?" Randy nodded. "You don't think there is someone out there for you to make you equally happy?"

"There was." Randy had told very few people about Penny. She'd been the love of his life when he'd been living at home. Reid knew about her, as did CJ. But he'd never told anyone else about his mate. She'd been in his heart since he'd first seen her when they'd both been about six.

"Your father should have gone to prison for killing her. And the fact that the governing body did nothing about him makes me want to find them all and drain them." Randy nodded, knowing that even if there was someone out there for him, he wasn't interested. He had plans for himself, and until he got his bucket list taken care of, there was no way he was looking either.

He was standing in his makeshift office when his phone rang. He didn't want to talk to Austin right now. After last night when he'd left the house, he was sure whatever he had to say to him was just going to piss him off more. He was well within his rights to leave the pack whenever he wanted.

"You going to be childish or listen to me?" Randy almost hung up but stopped when he heard Austin say his name. "We don't want you to leave us, can't you see that?"

"I can, but it doesn't change the fact that I have to." Randy thought it was becoming harder and harder to remember the reasons for leaving, but he was going to leave. "I have plans, Austin. More than I tried to tell you about last night. I want to see the world, and I can't do that from an office here in Ohio."

"Just give us another year. Your brother needs you now more than ever. And CJ. She will go nuts with one of her babies gone." CJ was like a mother to him, though she was only a few years older. But she'd saved his and Reid's life and he'd never be able to repay her. Austin too. "Please?"

Another year. He'd been leaving for two now, since he'd gotten his boards back. First, it had been to wait for his nephew to be born. And while he'd waited until his first birthday, then his second, Randy was growing more and more used to being a part of their lives. He wanted to live his own life, and staying here wasn't a part of his plan.

"I have to go. There's a client I have to see." He had to go to the hospital and see Miss Barker. They were moving her to her own room today and Phil had asked him to go and make sure it was smooth sailing for her. He'd be glad when she woke up. The poor woman was going to have to deal with so much when she did.

After hanging up the phone, he went to get his jacket. He'd never met the woman before and was actually looking forward to seeing her. Phil had said she was a real beauty. He was pulling into a parking space when his phone rang again. This time it was Phil.

"She's sort of awake." Randy asked him what that meant. "She's in and out of it, but when she's in, she keeps asking for her sister. No one has told her yet that she died."

"So I'm guessing you want me to tell her." Phil laughed. "I see. And how do I do that? Nice and easy? Or do I just rip the Band-Aid off and tell her that way."

"I'm sure you can figure it out. She's pretty upset according to the doctor, so I'm betting she might have figured it out by now. Oh, and while you're there, someone said that a new staff member has been lurking around her bed. Try to figure out if it's Carter. I'm betting he's read the fine print by now and knows that Miss Barker got all the money and everything else."

Randy told him he would. As he moved off the elevator, he saw the man. He had no idea why he knew it was someone that was there for the girl, but he did. Moving toward him at a slow, lazy pace, Randy was nearly by him when he grabbed him and tossed him against the wall. The gun with the silencer fell out of his pocket just as Randy snapped his head against the wall.

"And just what were you planning to do with that?" The man grunted but said nothing. "I'm betting you had a date with one of the people on this floor and I fucked it all up for you." Another snap of his head hitting the wall and Randy let him up. "What do you have to say for yourself?"

"Fuck you." Not a good answer, especially for the mood he was in. Slamming his head against the wall again, Randy asked the would-be killer once more. This time he got an answer, and it was just what he had expected.

"I was told she had to die and I was gonna be paid a good deal of money to help her along to her side of hell." That was too easy, and he nearly told him that when he looked up and saw Jodie. She winked at him. "I don't know who told me to do it. I was just told to come here and kill her and I'd get a shit ton of money. And if I did it this morning before she was settled, he'd double it."

"You know I had this under control." Jodie shrugged and smiled at him. "Why were you here? Checking up on me or something?"

"Nope. I had to come and see a man about a victim and saw you coming in. You looked like you wanted to kill somebody, and I didn't have time to come and bail you out. And so you know, I would have but I would have given you a hard time about it. So I thought I'd follow you." He nodded and moved when an officer came up behind him. "Sent some guys in to help out too. I figured you didn't have time to take him downtown and fill all the shitty paperwork that comes with it, and I asked this nice officer to come along and catch the bad guy for you."

"You could have asked." Again she shrugged. "I'm going to see the girl. Phil said she's awake. Wanna come with me?"

Jodie fell into step beside him. He was going to miss her. She was the perfect woman he thought his brother needed. Strong and full of piss and vinegar, as Nancy was always saying. He looked over at her and marveled again that she was simply not what she seemed.

"How about I give you the ability to read other people's minds?" He nearly missed a step when she asked him that. "It would save you a good deal of time."

Before he could answer her, she reached out and touched her fingers to his forehead. Suddenly, he found himself bent over with his hands on his knees. She'd knocked him for a loop.

"I didn't answer you." She laughed. "Fuck, Jodie, I don't want this shit. Take it back. I'm pretty sure I don't want to know what other people are thinking."

"Probably not, but it's too late now." He looked up at her. "You should also know that I gave you a little more, too. Shit, you're gonna hate me until you get used to it. Call it a…wedding gift."

"I'm pretty sure I gave you a wedding gift, and I don't want this. Seriously, take it back." She laughed as she moved down the hall. He wanted to strangle her. He was going to talk to Reid, who would take this mind-reading shit from him. At least he hoped he would.

The girl's room looked like someone had destroyed it. The bed had been turned over and there was liquid everywhere. The nurse on the floor was dead, and there was blood all over the floor and walls. A curtain had been pulled down, too, and there was a bloodied handprint on it as well. Whoever had killed her had not been very neat about it. He looked at Jodie when she cleared her throat.

"The girl, do you know where she was moved to?" He told her to the third floor. "That guy, do you think he would have done this?"

"He didn't smell like this room." That was enough for Jodie, who reached out and touched the girl's neck. Randy could smell the wolf in the room. And he was no one he'd had contact with.

"Her neck is broken, and then whoever it tore her throat out. Can you tell if it was wolf or something else?" She looked up at him when he didn't answer her. There was something else here, something he didn't understand. When she said his name, he looked at her.

"What if I told you that I can't tell what was in the room?" She looked around and then back at him as he continued. "There are several...tiger, panther, and vampire, but none of them were here with anger." He could smell that as well as he could their species.

"I can only smell antiseptic. And the blood. I've also called Reid. He's dealing with an emergency at the clinic and will be here soon." She stood up and went to the turned over bed. "Do you think this was destroyed because she wasn't here?"

They moved toward the door as one. It was time to check on Miss Barker. They were headed up the stairs to the room when an alarm went off. Putting on some speed, they burst through the door to the right floor just as a man fired a gun their way. Randy pulled his out and shot back just as Jodie shifted to her hawk. This was too dangerous to think about humans seeing them.

"Where the fuck is she?" Randy watched Jodie fly toward the man as he continued to yell down the hall. From where he was standing, Randy could see three bodies, all of them shot in the head, as well as a plethora of meds from a cart that was overturned. He didn't know this man either but reached out to his mind. Christ.

He wasn't here for Miss Barker but for his wife, who had tried to leave him. And he was going to kill everyone until he got to her. Some people didn't deserve to have someone in their corner. It was another reason why he'd never look for his mate.

Just as Jodie swooped down to his face, Randy came out from behind the door he'd been behind and shot the man in the head. He dropped like a stone. Randy didn't stop moving as he made his way to room three nineteen. Jodie shifted and was right on his heels. Reid joined them just before they entered the room.

Randy was stopped by one of the security officers before he could enter the room. They wanted his gun, but he wasn't ready to give it up just yet. Instead of giving it up, he hit him in the nose and moved around him. Some things were just too important to let go, he thought with a laugh.

~~~

Molly didn't have any way to defend herself, and even if she did have her gun, she wasn't all that sure she could have lifted it. The woman and man standing in front of her made her think even if she was armed, there was no way she could beat them. Closing her eyes against the wave of pain, she spoke to them.

"There isn't anyone in here but me. There was a nurse in here, but she ran out when the first shot was fired. I tried to make her stay, but she thought she was going to be able to help anyone that was hurt." Molly peeked at the woman when she spoke. "I'm sorry. I don't know if it's the drugs or what, but my hearing is a little off."

"I said there are four nurses in the hall that were killed. The shooter too. You hurt?" Molly just glared at her. "Okay, stupid question. Did the asshole out there hurt you?"

"No. No one in this hospital did." Molly looked at the man as he continued to stare at her. "The man out there, was he coming for me, too? Did he work for Carter?"

"Not that I'm aware of. Randy, my brother-in-law, and I were on our way to see you when the asshole in the hall started shooting at us. I'm Jodie Atkins and this is Reid Atkins, my husband." Jodie put out her hand, and Molly was embarrassed to see that she missed it twice before she was able to grasp it. The drugs were playing hell with her.

"My sister. Since no one will tell me shit, I'm assuming she died." Jodie looked at the man, and she did too. He nodded once before he spoke. Molly wasn't sure she wanted to hear what he had to say, but something he did say made her pause.

"Did you say that Carter is gunning for me? I'm pretty sure he's the one that shot me in the first place. He…Mary was leaving him." Her heart hurt for her sister, and she wanted the couple to go away so she could grieve. And plan. She was going to kill the motherfucker if it was the last thing she did.

"You can't do that." She looked at the man. "Kill him, I mean. If you do then you'll go to prison, and where will that leave you."

"What do I have left now?" She looked at the wall opposite to where they were. "I'd really like to be alone now. And if you could see your way to the nurse's station, I'd really like to have a pain pill about now or whenever things settle down around here." Jodie nodded, but the man just stood there. "Is there something else? Do you want to, I don't know, question me about the guy or something?"

"Not just yet. But you smell of wolf and panther, did you know that?" She looked at Jodie again, and Molly could see the humor there. Before she could tell them to get the hell out, someone else came into the room and Molly felt as if the room got considerably smaller. The man standing there looked like he'd just stepped off the pages of a centerfold and had sadly dressed again.

"Phil is on his way here." The name made her think of something but was gone before she could hold onto it. The man looked over at her, and she assumed he was Randy, the brother-in-law. "Miss Barker? How are you?"

"Just peachy. Can't you tell?" He grinned at her, and when he stepped forward, she had a feeling that he was going to take her hand, too, but he stopped suddenly and looked at her hard. "What?"

He didn't move, but he did glance at Reid. The exchange between the two men was profound, and Molly felt as if she had missed something...something really important. When he took a step back, she looked at Jodie, who was staring at her like she'd just discovered she was there. These people were just too strange to handle right at the moment.

"You can't be." Molly looked at Randy and tried to sit up. Okay, she'd had enough. It was time for these people to get the hell out. But he suddenly turned on his heel and left them. It was then that she realized she felt a little saddened for some reason. And that pissed her off. Molly looked at Jodie who moved toward her, taking out a Glock from the back of her pants.

"Here. I want you to have this. It's loaded and hot. I'll make sure you have another few clips within the hour." Molly took out the clip and let the round fly out when she snapped the muzzle back. She was putting it back together when she realized she was arming her. "There has just been too many people in this place wanting to shoot it to hell and back for you not to be armed. Like I said, you'll have extras before long."

"You don't think I'll shoot someone who pisses me off? I hate hospitals." Jodie agreed with her but said she trusted her. "If Carter or his men show up, will I be well within my rights to take him out if he comes near me?" Jodie nodded before answering her.

"Phil took care of a restraining order for you yesterday. And there are four guards outside your room right now. Try not to shoot them if you can help it." Jodie pulled on the cord that the nurse had told her about, and two nurses came in, one of them armed. "See these two? If anyone but them comes in before I get back, shoot them. I don't want you to take any chances."

Molly nodded, and the two nurses left. As soon as Reid moved out of the room, Jodie moved to the bed again. This time Molly was a little frightened. And when Jodie spoke, Molly wanted her to laugh, too, to tell her it was a joke.

"You're going to need to heal a good deal faster than you will on your own. I'm sorry about this." When her fingers touched her face, Molly felt herself tumble down a rabbit hole. There was no pain just…well, there was just nothing. And when she hit bottom, Molly settled into a deep sleep that made her think she was dead, too.

CHAPTER 3

Randy sat at his desk until well after the sun was at its highest part of the day. Phil had been by to see him twice before he'd gone and still he sat here. He looked at the table he'd been using as a desk because he'd told Phil there was no reason to waste money on a desk when he wasn't staying. He wasn't surprised to see Austin walk into the room a few minutes later.

"I guess Reid told you." Austin didn't say anything but leaned back in his chair. Randy had often wondered how a man his size could look relaxed all the time. "I'm not going to do shit about her."

"Perhaps if you told me what you're talking about I might be able to comment." Randy wasn't falling for it and said nothing. "Not going to say it? Well, that's fine. I'll talk. The girl, Molly, has been moved to the clinic for now. Jodie sped up her healing process so we could bring her here. I think she'll be safer on pack land than she will be anywhere else."

"Phil told me." Randy got up, took two bottles of water out of the small refrigerator, and handed one of them to Austin. "The man who shot up the third floor is dead. He killed five people before we got to him. His wife left him a week ago and he'd only just tracked down where she was. He'd beaten her up pretty badly, but it wasn't the first time. She'd filed for divorce three days ago. I'm guessing she is glad it's all over too."

Austin nodded as he took a long drink of his water. Randy waited for him to say something about the girl but he didn't. Not yet anyway. But he knew that he would, and Randy had already made up his mind to leave. In fact, he'd just bought his ticket to get the hell out of there before it was too late.

"Mom wants you to come over for dinner with her tomorrow. CJ and I are having dinner in town at a board meeting and she wants the company." Austin tossed the now empty plastic bottle in the recycling can. "And before you ask, no I didn't say anything about Molly. Mom and the baby are all alone and she said she misses you."

He missed her too. Nancy Force, like all her sons, had been like his family. Nancy had treated him and his brother like her own children. Randy found himself agreeing to go over before he thought about it. Austin handed him a thick file as he got up to get another water.

"I want you to look into that for me. I have this guy that wants to sell me his land, but I have a feeling it's more than that. Jodie said she'd never heard of him, and he was supposed to have the property on the other side of what we purchased from her a few years ago." Randy pulled up his real-estate contact and filled out the information he knew he'd ask for as Austin continued. "I have no idea why I have my suspicions about this, but I do."

His computer sang when he received a reply. Randy quickly read it over as he spoke to Austin. "With good reason I would say. The guy owes more than ten times what the property is worth in back taxes. The state is going to repo it in a few weeks, and whoever owns it will be hit with a huge fine too. And I'm sure will have to forfeit the land as part of the deal."

"Do you think we can get it from the state?" Randy loved looking things up and making them work. He moved through his contacts until he found the one he wanted and asked him about the property. He gave him the information he'd gotten from the taxation office in their town. In seconds he had another answer, as well as a request for some help with something from the guy at the state department.

"Carl said you can make a petition for it after the land is taken. He said he'd rush it through for you. Also," Randy grinned, "he wants to know if you're taking on any more pack. He said his alpha is retiring and he's only heard good things about you. I can vouch for the man. He's always been straight up with me."

Austin nodded. "I'll consider it. And will you put that through for me? I need to expand again. Last week we had a group of stragglers come in and we had to put them in tents again. Did you know that there are over nine thousand pack members here?"

"You'll need to break it up soon. If you don't, you'll get too big for the council and they'll start making waves about you paying dues." Randy didn't look up from his computer when he heard Austin laugh, but answered his friends question about the problem he had with a boss. "You should also know that I've looked into the land you asked about too. It has mineral rights on it. Carl said that if you don't make any noise about it, the man who currently owns it won't either. If he taps, then he might be able to get a loan to pay off the property before they seize it."

"What I need is another alpha to come in and take the property and some of the pack for me. I could help a man who wanted to do that." Randy nodded. It was a good idea and he could think of all sorts of ways Austin and this other guy would work too. "If the pack I have now were to divide down the middle, it would still be a lot for a new person, but I'd train them."

"You'd do a good job too. And there are ways for the two of you to make sure that no one comes into the pack without proper clearance. With a pack that big, for both of you it would have to have some leadership on a lower level, one that would bring you the larger problems while they fixed the smaller ones."

They talked for a few more minutes, and Randy filled out the paperwork for the land. If he was correct, Austin would get it for seven cents on the dollar and make all that back in one year after the minerals were tapped into. As he was just finishing up something more for Austin, Tristian came in. He really liked Jodie's father, but he knew when he walked in with a book that it wasn't going to go easy.

"I need you to help me with something. When are you leaving?" Randy looked at his ticket information and told him a week. It was the soonest he could get a flight out of their little town. And he didn't want to drive all the way across the state to go to a bigger airport.

"I have about five days. I want to be able to close up my apartment and do some…how the hell did you know I was leaving?" When he didn't answer him, Randy decided that the sooner he got out of there the better. These people were up in his business too much.

"I have my ways. And so you know, I think you're stupid if you think running from the girl will get you anything but trouble. She is gonna need you, and running isn't an Atkins style." Randy didn't say anything again, wondering how he'd gotten that information. He was going to kill Jodie when he saw her again. "I have this book. I'd very much like to lay out the laws in it in a semblance of order. You think you can do that?"

"I have five days. And whatever else you want will have to be taken care of with your daughter." He snorted. "She's mad at you again. What did you do now?"

"How the hell was I supposed to know that the new nanny hadn't been told about what they were yet? I just asked her if she was keeping a good eye on little Trist, but oh no, she had to get all fiery with me and I just let a little magic off." Tristian laughed. "Never seen a woman run that fast in all my life. And when she kicked off her shoes and took off across the yard, well it was all this old man could do not to chase her and see what else she'd do before she got to town. But I had the baby and I wasn't leaving him."

Tristan handed him the book, and power ran up his arms. Randy looked at Tristian, who looked as surprised as he was. Randy put the book on the table and rolled his chair back from it.

"Did you know it would do that?" Tristian shook his head. "Has anyone else touched this book and had anything happen to them?"

"Nope. I think you're the first. I thought you'd understand the book better than most, being a lawyer and all, but I didn't know it would accept you." Randy looked at the book, then at Tristian again when he continued. "Could have sworn all the spells in it were taken off. I guess it had a couple of its own."

"I guess." Randy put his hand out, and the book opened before he could touch it. He looked at Tristian when he stood up. "Tristian, if you're fucking with me, I don't think this is the least bit funny."

"I'm not doing it. I swear it." He moved to his side of the desk and looked at the page where the book opened too. "Didn't ever see that in there either, and I've looked at this book a hundred times in all the years I've had it. Who do you suppose she is?"

Randy knew. It was the cop...the woman from the bed. And her picture, or a drawing of her, was staring up at him as if she were standing in front of him. On the other page was him. And Randy wasn't thrilled when Tristian thought that was as funny as he apparently thought it was.

"You can bet that's your mate. Now when you see her you can nail her before she gets away." Randy didn't say anything as the pages moved again. This time when they stopped neither of them spoke for a long time.

"I know that place, do you?" Randy shook his head. "It's a plot of land about ten miles from where I was hurt all those years ago. I own it. It's one of the properties that I didn't sign over to your bother and my Jodie. What do you suppose it means?"

Randy didn't know, but the book slammed shut and when he opened it, Tristian told him it was the book he'd brought in, without the extras. Tristian told him what he wanted, and Randy was too freaked out to tell him no. The book had shown them both things, and he wasn't happy with what was there.

~~~

Molly knew the moment she opened her eyes that she was in a different place than she'd been before. First of all, this place was like a room in a very nice hotel, while the other had been a straight up hospital, and there were flowers everywhere here. When the door opened, she put her hand down on her hip and was surprised to find her gun still there.

"I'm Shari." The nurse stood there for several seconds before she moved toward her. She had a blood pressure cuff in one hand and a clipboard in the other. "I'm here to take your vitals. Is that all right?"

"Sure." Molly wasn't taking any chances and laid the gun on the top of the sheet so she could see it. "Just don't do anything stupid and you'll live longer."

Shari did her job and left soon after. Molly was sitting up in the bed a little more when she realized how much better she felt. Almost afraid to look at her body, she was glad when she was interrupted as the door opened again. This time Jodie and the man, Reid, stood there. He sat down in the chair and Jodie on the bed.

"You feeling better?" Molly nodded and put her hand around the butt of the gun. "You won't need it. Not that it would do you much good anyway. There isn't any silver in it. When I gave it to you, I didn't know you'd be coming here. I'll take care of that for you in a minute."

"And just where is here?" Neither of them answered, and she looked at Reid. "I demand to know where I've been taken. Or so help me, we'll test her theory as to whether it will do me any good."

"Force Clinic. And you're on pack land. Do you know what that means?" Molly shook her head as Reid continued. "A pack of weres, werewolves as a matter of fact, own this land. Officially it's wolves, but a lot of other species come here to run when they need to get away. Austin Force is the alpha here, and we, Jodie and I, live here. For the most part. We're away most of the...are you freaking out?"

"A little. What do you mean werewolf?" She had a feeling she was being punked but was afraid to ask if she was. She just knew that they were going to tell her that playing a joke on her was not what they were there for. "And I understand the word alpha, but not how it pertains to Austin or whoever he is."

"Yes you do. You understand a great deal. And the reason I know this is because you've seen things that you've tried very hard to rationalize and just couldn't." Molly nodded but said nothing as Reid continued. "Your boss, Martin, he's a wolf, too. He's been here to see you twice and is thinking of retiring here. His wife is a wolf as well."

"That can't be right. They have children. I was there when they were born." Reid laughed as he stood up. "Don't. I really will shoot you."

She hadn't picked up the gun and wasn't even sure she would use it on him if he did anything to harm her. She was so overwhelmed it was painful to her head. But he just pulled out his wallet and thumbed through it as he spoke softly. Molly had a feeling he was talking to her in the low, calming tones so she'd not shoot him. There was nothing for him to worry about. Right about now she was thinking she needed a stiff drink and a place to hide while she sucked on her thumb. She was too fucking overwhelmed to do much more than watch him as he handed her a picture.

"My wife and son when he was born. See? They look just like you." He handed her another picture. This one was of a silver and a white wolf. "My wife here and CJ. You'll meet her later. They're beautiful, aren't they?"

Her fingers were trembling when she handed them back. Sliding her hand under the sheet, she looked up at him. Reid just smiled. There was something so...she wanted to say calming, but he'd just told her he was a wolf and she didn't think calm entered the picture.

"Is Carter a real person? The reason I ask is because I thought he should be a snake or something. At least something that would slither along his belly as he caused harm." He shook his head and sat back down. "I'm freaking out. I mean...could you guys just go away? I mean, I think I can handle this better if I'm alone."

"I think not." Molly looked at Jodie as Reid left the room. She looked so serious even with the smile that only went to her mouth. Her eyes looked hard like she'd seen more than most people. "You're in danger, you know that, right?"

"I don't know why. Carter is getting what he wanted. My sister can no longer fight him on it." Molly looked away. "She was divorcing him. It's more than likely why he killed her. He was always a selfish prick. She was the fatted calf, so to speak."

Closing her eyes, Molly let the tears flow. She'd not done that since she'd heard about her sister. Mary, her kind and loving sister, was gone and now she was all alone. The door opened and closed after a few minutes, and Molly didn't bother looking. She just wanted to be left alone. Soon sleep took her.

Blood was everywhere. Her sister...someone had shot her and her eye was missing. Pain tore through Molly as she tried to reach her, but Mary kept moving further and further away from her until she was simply gone. When she looked up, a man was standing over her and he was pointing a gun to her head. Then suddenly he was a large, black wolf. A scream tore from her mouth as she sat up and pulled her gun. A man sitting there very still never moved as she tried to remember where she was. She realized she was pointing a gun at him when he looked down at it before speaking.

"I'm Phil Campbell." She nodded but didn't drop her gun. "I'm sure as the pain lessens you'll have less and less nightmares like the one you just had. I know that my pain, while there, is still hurtful, but it doesn't take my breath away. I understand you tried to save your sister by calling in the police."

"They were too late." He shook his head, and she frowned. "They told me that she died. I assumed it was at the scene or very close after."

"No. I spoke to her here at the hospital. She was alive when they brought her in but very close to death and asked for me. She and I had a long conversation just before she died." Molly lowered the gun, but she didn't let it go as Mr. Campbell continued. "She wanted me to give you a message. I do believe that is why she waited for me to come to her."

"She said you were her lawyer and that she trusted you. I don't." He nodded and smiled at her. "What are you? Mary said you were...not normal or something. I don't...that other couple, the Atkins, they said they were wolves. Are you?"

"They are, but I am not. I'm a vampire." She nodded. Okay, this was still a dream and she'd wake up soon. "You're not dreaming, Molly. May I call you that? I have a great deal of respect for what you do for a living. And now that you're awake, we can get down to business."

"What sort of...is the department suing me? I was an officer down. They knew that. I didn't use my job to get them there faster for my sister." He only smiled again and she saw his fangs. Molly didn't know why but thought he had done that on purpose. "Why are you here, Mr. Campbell?"

"Your sister left you everything." Molly was shaking her head as he moved his chair closer to the bed and started laying out papers on the little table. "She also had a message for you. She wanted you to live for her. I'm not sure what she thought you were doing prior to her death, but I'm reasonably sure she had her reasons."

"I was a hermit. She'd been telling me that for weeks. I love what I do and sort of worked a good deal more than I should have. She wanted me to date and to find...." Molly took a deep breath. "What do you mean she left me everything? I thought because Fuckwad and her were still married, he got it all."

"They weren't." Molly waited for him to continue, but he handed her a paper instead. It was a divorce decree. It was dated several months before her sister's death. Molly looked at the man.

"This isn't possible. She told me that day that she'd only just contacted you about this." He handed her another paper—this one was notes. A conversation between her sister and this man and the man she'd met at the hospital. Another werewolf, she assumed.

"She and I had an agreement. And when she died...was killed by someone, I decided to use my considerable power to make it happen so her husband got nothing." He took the papers and turned to somewhere in the middle before handing it back. "As you can see, she had made you her benefactor. She wanted you to have it all. If you'd like, I can continue to serve you until you—"

"Hang on." She looked at the divorce papers, then picked up the last sheath of papers. It was a will. Molly looked at the little tabs where Mary had signed, then at the pages that Mr. Campbell said she should see. "She didn't know what she was doing. I don't want all this. How much is it anyway? Never mind. I don't care."

"You should. Miss Ravenhall said that if you wanted to sell the house, she would be all right with that but thought you should live there for a time. She wanted you to get a feel for it before you let it go. I can have it sold for you in a few months, a year maybe. But if you wait on it, I'm sure I can get a better price. But like your sister, I think you should stay there. The locks have been changed, and a security team is in—"

"You're going too fast." Mr. Campbell sat down and looked at her. He wasn't mad, though she couldn't figure out why he wasn't. She'd hardly let him finish a statement since she'd woke up.

"Molly, your sister wanted you to live for her. She told me that. Her words were, 'tell Molly that she has to live for me.' She said it sounded like a line from one of her movies, but she was insistent about it. She wanted you to find a good man and have children. When I told her you might not make it either, she laughed and told me, 'She'll live. She's much too strong and stubborn not to, but how she lives will be what matters. Tell her to live. Not just breathe.'"

That sounded like something Mary would say, and Molly felt her tears start to flow again. Mr. Campbell handed her a tissue and waited while she tried to get herself under control. She had to think of something else and started talking simply to get her heart and mind under control.

"When we were small, Mary and I had this place we'd go to play. When I think back on it now, it's a small wonder we didn't get ourselves killed by running off on our own." The pain of what she'd said hurt, but she continued, "She would pretend to be all sorts of characters and I'd be her audience. She was amazing even back then."

"She was an amazing actress. I have seen all her movies." Molly nodded. "Molly, we can do this some other time. I know you must be hurting right now."

"I am. I don't know what to do. She was all I had." Not looking at him, she ran her finger over the borrowed gun and closed her eyes. "If you'll just give me the papers to sign, I'd like to get this over with. Then I want you to find a way to get rid of everything. There is nothing in that house that I'd want after Carter touched it."

The room was very quiet, and she turned to look at Mr. Campbell after a few minutes. He was gone and in his place was Randy Atkins. He frowned at her and sat down in the chair that Mr. Campbell was in.

"He asked me to come and finish this for him. The sun is beating down on him, he said." She nodded as he handed her the papers again. "I'm not sure where he left off, but if you can tell me, I'll get things going."

"Are you really a wolf?" He looked at her and nodded. "Show me." She had no idea why she'd asked him to do that, but he didn't move for several seconds. When he stood up, she almost told him to forget it. But he took off his jacket and laid it at the foot of her bed.

"I'll only morph my arm if that's okay with you." She nodded as he took off his cuff links and handed them to her. When his fingers brushed over her palm, her breath caught and she looked up at him. He grimaced. "I'd rather we didn't touch. It's very difficult to be with you now."

"Why?" He didn't answer her as he rolled up his sleeve. When his lovely grey shirt sleeve was up to his elbow, she looked at his arm and watched as hair, dark and thick, sprouted there. Then his hand changed. Where his fingers had been, now there was long, sharp claws and his hand was a thick paw. She wanted to be terrified of what he was showing her, but more than anything she wanted to touch him.

"I'm your mate. Did anyone tell you that?" She shook her head and watched as he changed back to a regular person. "My wolf knows who you are to us and he wants me to mark you. I'm not going to. We have to stay apart or the power of your scent will make me do things to you that neither of us will want."

"Like?" Randy pulled his sleeve down and then pulled on his jacket. She still had his cuff links and put them on the table when he pointed to it. He picked them up and put them into his pocket. When he started gathering up his briefcase she'd only just noticed he'd had, she asked him again.

"Like he wants me to fuck you. Hard and fast. Take you from behind and mark you as he comes deep inside of you." Her body seemed to catch fire as he continued, his voice hard and unforgiving. "Then as a man, I'd want to do the same. Eat your pussy until I've had my fill of you, then slam my cock into you until I fill you up. Then again when you come, I'll want to sink my teeth into your creamy flesh and taste your spiked blood, filling you with my essence so no other male will come near you." He leaned down to her, and she felt his hot breath on her lips and licked them. "Tell me to leave you now, Molly. Tell me or I'm going to kiss you."

Her breath seemed to sear her lungs, her heart rate had tripled, and she could feel her body getting ready for him. A stranger, she kept telling herself, and it did little good. She wanted him as much as she needed her next breath. Even as breathless as she was, she told him to leave.

"Too late." His mouth took hers almost as soon as his words left his mouth. Not in a simple kiss as she had expected but a taking. He devoured her mouth; his tongue touched her in places that made her body pulse with need. When his fingers curled in the back of her head and he tilted her head, she moaned. Randy seemed to touch her deep inside of her body, and she wanted...no, she *needed* more. But before she could pull him on top of her, have him do all the things he'd thought to threaten her with, he jerked away from her.

"Stay away from me and I'll do the same. We cannot let this take us." Molly wanted to point out she'd wanted him to leave but knew he'd know it for the lie it was. Before she could say anything, not even sure what it might have been, he was gone and she was all alone.

"Mother fuck." She laid back on the bed and tried to reason what had happened just now. But her fingers on her swollen lips had her wondering if a kiss from him could make her feel this way, then what the hell sex would be like.

CHAPTER 4

Randy stomped around his apartment for an hour before he realized he needed to take a long run. He reached for his brother and asked if he could run on his property and was told to go ahead.

"You okay? You're sounding a little on edge." Randy told him that he was fine. And he was pretty sure that his brother knew that he wasn't. *"I'm just getting excited about leaving. It's only in a few days."*

He had been working on the laws and bylaws from the book when he'd been asked by Phil to come back and make sure that Molly Barker had all she needed. He'd made sure of that all right. He'd nearly fucked her on the hospital bed.

"Yeah, we're going to have to get together before you go. I have some things I want you to do for me." His brother was his only family and if he wanted something done for him, Randy knew he'd do it. At all costs. *"Did you know that woman left the hospital today?"*

"She did?" Randy paused in getting into his car to think of how delicious she'd tasted and tried to squash that thought. *"I had to have her sign some papers today. She didn't say anything about leaving."*

He'd not done that either. All he'd been asked to do was have her sign the bank card and to have her sign a

51

contract making Phil's firm her lawyer until she found one of her own. All he'd managed to do was taste her, and now he couldn't get out of his mind how soft and yet firm she'd been when he touched her.

"She left without being released. The nurse we had watching her said she went in to take her vitals again and she was packed up. Said she'd called a friend of hers to come and get her. It was that new guy that is retiring from her station. I think his name is Martin something. I guess he's pledging to Austin in the morning."

She was with another man was all his mind could accept at the moment. Instead of going to his brother's, he found himself going to her apartment. It was a long drive but maybe he'd be calmer for it when he got there. For some reason Randy doubted it, but he was hoping so. He told Reid that he had to do something and would meet him later. An hour later he was pulling up in front of her shabby apartment building.

There was no security, and as soon as he walked up to her front door he knew that she was not going to be staying there again. He could smell the urine coming from the second floor as he made his way to the fourth. The elevator, he'd been told, had never worked.

Randy moved down the hall to her apartment. He'd had to find her address when she'd been named in the will even though they all knew where she was. Randy had no idea why he'd remembered it but was glad now that he had. Looking around, he pressed hard against the doorframe, and it gave too easily as far as he was concerned.

The room he walked into was in direct contrast to the rest of the building. Where it was run down and dirty, this room, her living room, he supposed, was spotless and full of dark earth tones. After closing the door as best he could, he walked around the room.

The couch was a deep red, almost blood red, with pillows of every hue of brown he'd ever seen. He thought of fall when he looked at them together, and the throw on the back looked like one that CJ used to have sent to him at college. Like the one she'd brought them the first time he'd seen her and Austin.

There was a smallish television that sat on an old table and an old VCR. He had no idea they even made them anymore. But her collection of tapes made him smile. She watched the same sort of movies he liked. Classics as well as murder mysteries. There were plants in the window as well as on most of the tables around the room. Picking up the watering can, he walked to the kitchen to fill it.

The kitchen was as lovely as the living room. Here she'd used dark blues and darker golds. He loved the mixture, and while the can filled he opened her cabinets to see what she ate. He nearly burst out laughing when he saw the nine boxes of sugary sweet cereal all lined up. There was also a box of ramen noodles and nothing else. So she wasn't a cook. He was. Before he could let that train of thought go on, he turned off the water and started filling the pots in this room first. He was nearly finished with the living room when he felt someone coming down the hall toward him.

The man wasn't thinking of harming anyone, but he was armed. The ball bat could hurt Randy, sure, but he was more concerned about the fact that the man was pissed off about the rent being late. Randy was standing there with his hands free when the man pushed the door open. He'd have to thank Jodie for the little extra she'd given him at the hospital.

"Whatcha doing here? The girl that lives here lives alone, and you don't look like her type anyway." Randy nodded and moved into the man's mind a little deeper to see what sort of type he thought Molly had. Thankfully he'd never seen her with another man but was still pissy.

"I'm her friend. I've come by to collect a few things for her and to water her plants." The man looked at the door. "It was like that when I got here."

He looked at the door and started cussing. "There was this fancy pants man here about two hours ago looking to see her, but I told him she hadn't been in. Then I got this call I was waiting on and he might have slipped by me." Randy nodded and looked for what the man might have looked like as the landlord continued. "Her rent is past due. She is good about paying on time and I...I was worried about her being a cop and all."

"She was hurt not long ago. That's why I'm here." He reached for his wallet slowly. "If you tell me how much she owes and how much you think it will cost to fix the door, I'll take care of that now. I'm also going to have someone come in and pack her things up. She will be staying with me for a while."

He nodded and told him a price. Randy knew that it was much higher than her rent was and way more than it would cost to fix the door, but he paid the man and was handed a key when he told the man he'd need one. He wasn't sure what he'd do with it once the door was fixed, but he felt better about having something that would show he was coming back. Randy knew that Molly was going to be pissed when she found out how high handed he'd been.

Randy pulled out his cell phone and called a few of his pack members in to help him move her. She couldn't stay here even if she wanted to. Carter would return and if she was here, Randy didn't think anyone would help her out if she needed it. Within an hour he had the plants put on the counter and most of her kitchen packed up when three trucks pulled up out front. And two hours later, the apartment was emptied of everything, including the left over beers he'd paid his buddies with. They were on their way back to his place when his phone rang.

"What do you think you're doing?" He wasn't sure who he was talking to and waited. They'd either give him more information so he could answer or he'd have to ask who it was. "This is Molly Barker. My landlord just called me and said someone is moving my things out. And when he described you to me, I had to...what are you doing moving me out of my own place?"

"Carter sent a man here to kill you." That shut her up. For all of about ten seconds. And when she started telling him she could handle him herself, he cut her off. "And how would you do that? Shoot him? I doubt very much you'd get away with that. And the goon he sent for you, the man was a wolf too. Do you have any idea what he would have done to you had he smelled me on you?"

"Smelled you on me? What the hell are you talking about? You know what, I don't care. You stop what you're doing right now and put my things right back where you got them. And if one thing is broken, I'm going to sue you." He could almost see her with her hands on her hips giving him orders. Randy had no idea why he thought that was funny, but he laughed.

"I'm finished and we're about ten minutes from the pack house right now. By the way, I'd thought you'd be at the apartment when you left the hospital. Where did you go?"

Her voice cracked, and he knew that she'd gone to her sister's home, now her home. "I wanted to see if there was anything here I wanted. It smells like her. And there are her clothes in her closets that she wore the night before she…. I was at her premier with her and we'd had such a good time."

Randy pulled off at the next exit to go to the house. It was a little closer to the pack house than he was right now and told the others to go on. He knew that they'd put her things in the barn or somewhere to store them. He had to go to her.

"I saw her last movie. Your sister could light up a screen like nobody else could." He pulled up the long drive and waved to the security officer that came out just as he pulled up. "I'm almost to you, Molly."

"Don't bother. I'm leaving now anyway." He stopped the car in the front of the garage and got out. Christ, this house was bigger than the one that he and his brother had bought a few years ago. She was just coming out when he got to the steps.

"This is a lovely home." She nodded and held what looked like frames closer to her chest. "Would you like to show me around?"

"No." She didn't move, and neither did he. He wanted to pull her into his arms but knew that the moment he touched her it would be lost. Hell, he thought, it was already. "My brother and his wife have a large home, too. It's their kitchen that I love. Do you cook?"

"You know I don't if you were at my apartment. Are my things being put back where they were before you barged into my life and moved them?" He shook his head. "Are you always this pushy? And do you generally get your way? I'm not a pushover, so you know."

"Yes to both questions. And I'm well aware that you are not a pushover. You're very...scrappy, as my friend would say." He took a step toward her, then another. "Do you have any idea how much I'd like to kiss you again? Take your mouth with mine and see if what I tasted there was real?"

"You said for me to leave you alone. Maybe you should listen to your own advice." He was pretty sure she was right but took another step up and was on the same level as she was. "You're not going to touch me. I don't want you to at any rate."

"Don't you, love?" He ran his fingers down her cheek and watched her eyes close. She was his, and his body wanted her. Randy felt his wolf run along his skin and knew that he wanted his mate, too. "Molly, can I kiss you again?"

"No." He moved closer when she took a step back. He could smell her. She was slightly aroused, and he wanted to make her scent a part of the air around them. "You should really leave now. I've got things to do. And you're just...too much for me to have to deal with. On any level."

"I don't think I can...leave you, I mean. For as much as I want to, I don't think I'm going to be able to." He heard the car pull up behind them and he turned and shoved her behind him. His wolf snarled along his skin this time, and Randy let him go. Whoever was there had interrupted them and they were going to pay. Austin got out of his car slowly and stood still with his hands out. His brother stood on the passenger side and didn't move either.

"I heard that you were here and wanted to talk to you." Randy snarled and felt his hackles rise. "Randy, you're scaring your mate. Perhaps you can turn to her now and assure her that you're not going to kill her. I won't move."

Randy turned and saw that Molly was holding a gun on him and had backed as far from him as she could get without going into the house. Her pictures lay scattered and broken on the landing in front of her. He heard Austin tell her not to run. Randy found he wanted her to. Just so he could run her down and take her.

"I can't talk to her. We've not…Christ, I never meant to scare her, but you startled me." Austin told him that he'd tell her whatever he wanted. *"Tell her it's me."*

"Molly, honey, put the gun down. You saw Randy shift, so you know that it's him. Just put the gun away and he'll shift back when I find him something to wear."

"He is a wolf. He really is a fucking wolf." Randy watched her face as she spoke. He wanted to shift for her again but would be naked and wasn't sure what she'd do to him if he was suddenly a man again. "Tell him to make himself a man again. I don't want to have to shoot him if he attacks me."

"He won't attack you. I swear he won't. If you'd just lower the gun, we can all go into your house and talk." Randy glanced over his shoulder to his brother and noticed that while his arms were spread out, he was moving toward them. He spoke to her slowly and in low, soothing tones "Molly, you have to trust me on this, he's not going to be able to ever hurt you."

"Why not?" Randy wanted to tell her why he couldn't hurt her but watched her face again. He wanted to see what her reaction was when she was told again she was his mate. Austin explained to her that it was in their DNA to never harm their females. That they were as precious to him as their own bodies.

She stood staring at him without saying anything. When she lowered the gun, he thought about moving toward her, but didn't when Austin told him to wait. It was the hardest thing he'd ever done.

"I don't think she'll hurt me now. She'll be reasonable." Austin told him he was going to kill him when this was over and there was no such thing as a reasonable female of any species. *"Austin, what am I going to do now? I have all these plans and they don't include a mate. I want to be free, go where I want, do what I want."*

"And how is she going to make a difference in that?" Randy didn't know but said nothing to him. *"You think that CJ and I just sit around the house just waiting for one of you guys to come by? We do lots of stuff. And the great part of it is, I can share all those times with her. Nothing has changed in my life in a negative way. I love her and want to be with her."*

"I don't love Molly any more than she does me. I just want her." Which was true, he did want her. *"She is going to be a cop, and I want to be the best lawyer I can be. But not here."*

"I don't see the problem." Randy did. All sorts of them. When she said something, he looked at her. She was his if he wanted her. Molly would be his mate and carry his children if he would want it. The problem was, he didn't have any idea if he did or not. He looked at his brother, who was less than three feet from them.

"Ask her if there is anything in the house I can put on. I know you wanted to talk to us both, but I can't do it as a wolf." Austin asked her, and she said there were Carter's things still in the house. She turned to unlock the door just as another car pulled up. This time it was Tristian and he looked so excited Randy knew he'd seen the wall.

~~~

They were pinning things to a large piece of plywood when she returned to the office. Molly didn't want them there, but Tristian, another vampire, begged her to let him show what Randy had done so far. She had gone to the kitchen to find them something to drink and had started talking to her sister's butler.

"Will you be staying, Miss Molly? The staff is up in arms as to what we're to do. Mr. Ravenhall said that we were all to be replaced. Then we were told that he was no longer allowed on the premises." She wanted to tell him that she didn't want the house either, but he looked so afraid that she lied to him.

"I want you to stay, all of you. I'm not sure how this works yet...." She looked up at him after sitting in the kitchen chair. "There are others here that are going to expect me to run this household like I know what the fuck I'm doing. I'm not even sure where my clothes are, much less my furniture. I have more money now than I've ever seen even on a huge bust, and I have a staff that needs me to make decisions for them."

She didn't mention that she'd had to find a pair of pants and a shirt for the man who'd changed into a wolf not an hour ago, and now he was in the office her sister had used, talking to an alpha as well as two vampires. What did she even feed those people?

"We'll make sure you don't fail, miss. We'll make dinner for them and we'll...miss, are you aware that those men in there are not human either?" She looked at Shawn and nodded. "Good, this will make things so much easier. I'm a panther, and my wife is as well. Are you aware of that?"

"No." He smiled at her and told her not to worry. "I don't think I would know where to begin about worrying, Shawn. Right now I can't tell who is what and what I'm supposed to do with them." She'd been introduced to

Shawn Charles when she had first visited her sister. She had a feeling, though she wasn't sure why, that her sister had not cared for the older man. She thought it was because Carter had hired him.

"We'll get there." Shawn told her they'd bring in refreshments in a bit and sent her to the office again. When she sat down, she looked at the board as they put things in what to her seemed a random order that made little to no sense. Or at least she thought that was what they were doing. Maybe that's what they were doing, just pinning things on it to get ready. She also noticed that another man, a vampire she'd been told, had shown up. Myles Kramer was a large, scary man, but she felt as if they had a good deal more in common than she and Randy did.

"I don't think those are lining up correctly. Some of it's missing." They all turned to her, and she flushed. "I'm sorry. I don't know what I'm talking about."

Myles, a man she thought she'd met before, turned to look at her. She could see his fangs, too, and wanted to ask him about them, but right then, Shawn came in.

"What is missing? I know you would see things we can't. Fresh eyes and all." She stood up and went to the board. Myles stepped back when she stood in front of the board. It looked like they were making a list of rules and the consequences if they were broken. She looked at the one that was about murdering one of their own kind.

"I'm assuming you mean like a wolf murdering a wolf, not humans?" Myles smiled and nodded. "Okay. Why would one murder his own kind?" She turned when no one answered and they were all looking at Randy. "Did you do this to someone?"

"No. They're waiting on my permission to speak to you. I don't know how to answer that." She cocked her head at him, and he laughed. "For some reason I think if I told you that you couldn't talk to them directly, you'd do it anyway just to piss me off."

"I could care less if I piss you off." She turned back to the board and tried to ignore the men behind her. She knew that Randy was close to her and her entire body seemed to like it. "There are just black and white rules here. You've left no room for gray. There has to be gray."

"Why?" She glanced at Myles and decided that for some reason he knew the answers but wanted her to figure them out for them. "I like rules. They make my job easier, and it runs much smoother when I know them going into a situation. If I know that this man or that one has killed, I know that it is well within my rights to drain him."

"Yes, but what if?" She turned to look at anyone but Randy. He was looking at her again, and she felt all mushy inside when he did. And Molly was not mushy. "*What if* is a game I play when I'm out working. What if you know that this person, this species, killed this other of his kind? But what if he did it because he was…?"

Myles grinned. "What if he had touched his mate knowing that it's against the laws of any of our kind and did it just to piss him off. And it got out of hand when the second man kept it up."

"There's a rule for that?" Myles nodded and stood up to come near her. "Why would anyone care if another male touched their whatever?"

"Mate. And it's a super thing." He ran his finger down her arm, and she heard someone growl. She knew before she looked around that it was Randy. And she also knew that Myles was doing this on purpose.

"Get away from her." The voice was very close, almost too close, and when she was pulled back against a chest, her entire body seemed to react to his touch like it was chocolate and she was ready to binge. "You keep this up and I'm not going to be able to resist taking you up to the first bedroom I find and claiming you."

"You don't want me." Randy's breath on her neck had her moaning, and she wanted to turn in his arms and touch him. "You should leave now before you do something you're going to regret. I won't have you blaming whatever happens on me."

"I want to. Hell, I need to turn and leave you, but I can't. Your body, your scent, it's calling to me." Molly did the hardest thing she'd ever done and stepped away from him. His growl when he reached for her made her body scream at her to go back, so she took another step away and turned to look at him.

"It's time for you all to go." She looked at Myles and then at Austin and Reid. Tristian stood up and stared at the rest of them as if he expected them to do as she'd said. "I want you to stay away from here, all of you. I...if I need anything, which I have no idea what that would ever be, I'll contact the police."

Randy stood there for a long time. She wondered if he'd leave or touch her again. Molly knew that if he did touch her she'd be lost, and so would everything she'd worked so hard to make work for her. When Austin stood up, she felt his anger and wasn't sure what she'd done to piss him off and really didn't care. As soon as he and the rest, along with Randy, walked out, she turned to look at Myles.

"You did that on purpose." He nodded. "Why? Why would you make him do something he doesn't want to do? Some sort of man thing? Or is it a vampire thing you're trying to show me?"

"Neither. It's a bonding thing. Once he has you, and I'm sure he's on the edge, you'll be safer and so will he. Right now he's a time bomb ready to go off at anyone or anything. He needs you." She looked at the door Randy had left, but then back at Myles when he continued. "When he comes to you, and I've no doubt that he will, will you accept him? And all that he is?"

"No." He shrugged and picked up his jacket. "Why do you care if he does or not? Aren't you and wolves supposed to be like these mortal enemies or something?"

"Usually. And the reason I care? It's because he is my family. Austin and CJ raised him when he was still a pup. Reid, Randy's brother, and him would be dead without them. When he comes to you—and as I said, he will—nothing will stop him. Not even you if he tries to make you stay away from him."

She sat down when she was alone. The board was there and she stood up to look at it, trying to think of anything but what Myles had told her. Randy would find her and he'd fuck her. And she knew that she'd be no better off with a mate or whatever they were than her sister had been with Carter.

CHAPTER 5

Carter was going to have to go to greater lengths than he'd anticipated to get into the house. He had money stashed in it and some jewels. But mostly he wanted back inside because it was his. And the fucking cunt had no right to toss him out like she had.

Mary had been a nobody in high school. She'd been too shy and backward most of the time around the campus, but she'd really shown when she'd been in a play or something. Not that he'd gone to any of them, but he'd been told so. He and his friends had wanted to get a piece of her but never got the chance. Carter decided that he'd be the one to fuck the bitch. It wasn't until graduation that things started to fall into place for her and apart for him. He still blamed that on her and had wanted her sister to pay as well. Carter needed Mary and her fame more than he needed his next breath. And still did.

He'd been a high school quarterback, all pro, and had colleges looking at him like he was going to be their saving grace. He'd eaten it up too, letting them woo him and tell him what they were going to give him. Then one night after leaving a party a little too drunk, he'd lost it all. Even now, all these years later, he knew that had he not gotten caught, he would have been famous. Endorsements alone would have given him all he wanted.

He'd wanted her...not because she was anything special, but because she told him no. And as far as anyone knew, no one had had her yet either. It was a dare that had gotten him drunk at the party. Not that he'd needed the alcohol to go after her but because she hated it...that and any form of drugs, which included smoking a little pot before a game. Few girls had ever turned him down, and all of them he'd had anyway. Carter liked the feelings drugs gave him during sex. If a girl got hurt, she'd not be on his list the next time he wanted to fuck someone. There were plenty of girls who never told him no. Carter didn't like it when he was told he couldn't have something he wanted.

Mary had been at the party with her sister, the lying fucking bitch Molly. The two of them were like looking at wet dreams and held a promise that said when they gave it up, it would be well worth the wait. He wanted them both. But he'd tangled with Molly once before that night and had crossed her off his list. She was simply too mean and much too butch for his taste anyway. But not Mary.

Mary had turned him down so many times that when he would walk up to her, she would put out her hand and tell him no. He wouldn't even have to ask her anything. He wanted to mark her off too, but his buddies got wind of her rejection and he had to make her his just to prove he could have her. It was simply too good of an angle to ignore. Then one of his friends had bet him he couldn't get into her pants that night. That set the stage.

Mary was coming out of the bathroom when one of his friends had tried to get her to go back in with him. It was the plan they'd come up with. He'd try to rape Mary and Carter would go in and be the big guy. It was working perfectly until Molly showed up. Carter had wanted to be her knight in shining armor, but her sister had been. Molly had knocked his friend out and had taken her sister out of the house before Carter could get his wits about him. Drugs also made his thinking slower, he thought. Carter followed them as they were making their way back to their home by walking.

"Get in the fucking car." He'd hung his head out of the car as he'd been driving by them. Another girl, her name still eluded him, had joined Molly and Mary, and she told him to go home. "I said for you to get into the car. I'm taking you home."

"Fuck off. We're less than three blocks from home." Molly put her arm around her sister as she continued. "You should know that I'm going to tell your coach in the morning. You're a fucking drunk."

Mary was crying, and he'd stopped his car and moved toward them. Carter was never really sure how it had happened, but his car started moving as he approached the girls. He should have tried to stop it, but he didn't want to hurt himself before the last game of the season, and the car, like his shoes and coat, didn't really mean anything to him as they were a gift from a college, one he had already decided not to attend. The car was so last year.

But the girl, whatever her name was, had slipped and the car had run over her before she could be helped up. Carter had watched in horror as her blood splattered over the three of them and her screams were suddenly cut off. He'd never sobered up so quickly in his life. And wiping the blood from his face, he looked at the girls standing there with him.

"And then she married me." It wasn't as easy as that and he was well aware of it. He'd blackmailed Mary by lying to her…had told her that he was remembering so much of that night a few weeks after it happened, and that her sister, Molly, had pushed the girl in front of the car. All lies, of course, but Mary loved her sister.

"You know that's not true. We all tried to get away from you." Molly had been away at college and was not there to defend herself. Mary was all alone and he was going to make her give him what he wanted.

"So you say. But who do you think they'll believe? A girl from the wrong side of the tracks or a big famous football star like me?" But he wasn't famous, at least not like he'd planned to be. He was now the town joke. He'd found out that morning that all his hard work was for nothing. His future career as a football star was down the fucking drain. All thanks to Molly and Mary.

Molly had done just what she said she'd do and had gone to the coach and told them he was drunk. When that hadn't worked, she'd gone to the papers. The police, who had that night told him that he had to keep his mouth shut, had hidden that he'd been a minor and drunk when the accident happened. Once the paper broke with the news, everything came out, including the fact that most of the colleges that had been wanting him had paid him something in return for him promising to sign with them. He'd never had so many things change in a heartbeat as he had in that crowning moment. Even his dad, the biggest supporter of him taking what they'd offered him, and who had—on more than one occasion—bought him his beer, had kicked him out of the house.

"I'll tell you what…you say you'll marry me and I'll make sure that your sister stays out of jail. Her scholarship won't be revoked and she won't have to pay back all that money they gave her to go to school." He was proud that he'd remembered that Molly had graduated from high school two years before him, though she was three years younger, and had won a chance to go to college because her grades had been that good. Mary looked at him as if he made her skin crawl. He didn't care. He'd have her, divorce her, and be able to have the bragging rights that he'd fucked the ice queen.

"And she'll never hear about this?" He nodded. Like he gave a shit if she heard about it. He told her that he'd keep his mouth shut so long as she was his wife. "I'll do it. I hate you and always will, but I'll do it."

Three weeks later they were married. And a week after that Mary Ravenhall got her first speaking part in a motion picture. After that, things went from good to fucking fantastic, and he found he loved being married to a famous actress almost as much as he loved fucking one.

"And now she's dead and I got nothing after all the times I had to work on not hitting her where the camera would see it." He laughed at his own joke and wished he'd popped her a few more times in the face for all the good it had done him. Mary had been so good at hiding what he'd done to her until that last time Molly the cop had come home and found her sister in the hospital.

"You fucking bastard." He'd been in his office, a special little place that he would watch porn all day and suck up his wife's money by buying whatever came up on the shopping networks. Molly had crashed into his office and caught him getting a blowjob while watching his favorite DVD. His secretary was just about to get her throat lubed when Molly came in the room.

"I'm about to come. Can you give her a minute?" The woman at his dick had looked up at him, and he pressed her back to his cock. "Suck it or get fired. Up to you."

Molly pulled her gun out, put it to his head, and told the girl to leave. The woman got up quicker than she'd gone down on him, and Carter felt his cock grow soft when Molly put her gun to his balls.

"You're going to tell me why you're hitting my sister, or so help me I'll redecorate your office with your balls."

Carter had never hated her as much as he did at that moment. Not only had she caught him at his fun, but she had left the door open so now everyone stood watching. Two of the people who worked for him even had the nerve to laugh at him. He ordered them to get out, but Molly only laughed.

"They don't answer to you, do they? No one does. Just my dear sister Mary." He glared at her as two more people walked in. "Shall I call my sister here? Oh wait, she's in the hospital. And you put her there. Did you really think that I'd not find out that you beat her up whenever the mood struck you?"

"She gets what she deserves. I can't help it if she likes to get knocked around a little." The gun barrel felt as if it were a part of his body when she rammed it harder into his nuts. "You know that fucking hurts. And when I'm finished here, I'm going to make you pay for this."

"Oh, you're finished. I talked to my sister, you motherfucker. You actually threatened her into marrying you?" He looked at her and wondered how much more his dear soon-to-be-dead wife had told her. But Molly knew it all. "And I'm going to tell everyone I know what a sadistic fuck you are. I've even talked her into divorcing you."

"She's tried that before. I know more dirt on people than they even know. I've stopped it before, and I'll do it every time. She's fucking mine and what she has is mine. Till death us do part."

Molly laughed. He felt as if she were raking her nails down a chalkboard and wanted to beg her to stop. But he never begged anyone.

"I got news for you, fuckwad. She's not only going to go through with it, I'm going to help her get you out."

That had been ten days before he'd had her killed. They were supposed to take out Molly as well. In fact, she was the one he really wanted dead, but she'd survived. Now, due to some twist of fate, he had lost it all again. And once again, it was Molly's fault.

"Mr. Ravenhall, there's a call on line one." He reached for the phone just as his secretary closed the door behind her. He was glad now that he'd had this little enterprise set up before he'd hired a gun for his wife and sister-in-law. It was keeping him afloat until he was back to his home. He'd stashed away the money to keep this going, but that, too, was running low now that he didn't have an endless supply of money at his fingertips.

"Someone has moved into your house." He tried to wrap his mind around what his man was talking about when he continued. "Yesterday there was a few trucks pulling up and they were there for some time. I thought they were moving your shit back in that had been taken out the week before. Then today, a delivery truck came by from a mattress store. I asked the driver before he left the grounds and he said that he was making a delivery to the new owner. He wouldn't tell me their name. Did she sell already?"

"How the hell should I know? That's what I pay you for." Carter got online and tried to find the records for the courthouse that would give him the information he wanted. He was ready to scream when Archie, his go to man, spoke again.

"I just looked. She hasn't sold anything, but according to records, she has had her name put on the deeds. Her lawyer, a Phil Campbell, filed the papers this morning."

"Well, I want them unfiled." Even to his ears he sounded stupid. "Find this fucker for me and bring him to my office. I want to have a few words with him on the...wait. What did you say his name was?"

As Archie repeated the name twice, Carter dug out his divorce papers. Right on the bottom was the name Phil Campbell. The motherfucker was taking everything from him. He tried to calm his heart rate when it felt as if a rhino was sitting on his chest but knew it was futile. Everything was going to shit again. He had to reach for his pills as he worked harder at slowing his heart down. Some days, and especially lately, it was getting harder and harder to keep his heart from exploding in his chest.

"I want you to get this guy and bring him to my office today. Tell him...fuck, I don't care what you tell him, just get his ass here." He was ready to slam down his phone when he thought of Molly living in his house. "And find that bitch Molly. I want her here yesterday."

He put the phone down when Archie said he'd do it. Not "I'll try," but he'd do it. Carter was sure he would. But right now, he was trying his best not to die. He should have listened to the doctors when they told him to lose weight and to quit the drugs. Now they told him he needed a new heart or he'd be dead in a few years anyway. That, too, had gone to shit when his money had been taken from him. Mother fuck, he hated the Barker women.

He was closing his eyes when he heard his secretary come into the room. She would know better than to disturb him, and when the blinds were closed, he felt the blanket fall over his body. She deserved a raise for how well she cared for him. He wouldn't give it to her, but she probably should have had one. As he waited for sleep to take him, he thought of all the ways he was going to make Molly pay.

~~~

Randy was sitting in the kitchen of Molly's home when she came in. He looked at the butler, Shawn, but saw that he was on his own. Randy and the big man had run together on his brother's property a few times long ago. Who knew that they'd be in the same house like this again?

"I thought I told you to not come back here. Or have you forgotten since yesterday?" Molly moved to the refrigerator and pulled out a jug of water. She didn't offer him a glass, so he got up and got himself one before pouring a full glass of the cold liquid.

"I'm not sure me leaving is such a good idea. I wanted to talk to you about the man who's been watching the house. Were you aware that he knows you ordered a mattress?" He saw her pause with the glass halfway to her mouth, but she covered well enough. He doubted that she'd be able to when he told her the rest.

"I didn't want to sleep on the bed that Carter used. He and my sister never slept in the same bed, and he had insisted on the master suite. I'm getting rid of the furniture in there, too. Would you like it?" He shook his head, and she nodded. "Too bad. I'm sure as a bully like him, you'd enjoy the ugly stuff."

He didn't rise to the bait but countered with his own. "I sort of like your bed you had at your apartment. It's big enough for the two us to have some very good times, and when I want to have more fun, I could tie you to the bedposts to have my way with you."

Randy didn't look at Shawn when he dropped something in the sink. It was all Randy could do not to pull her into his lap and kiss the shocked look from her face. She set her water down and put her hands into her lap. He reached out to her mind and saw that she was thinking of him tying her to the bed. He sent her images of his own to add to hers. When she looked at him, he knew the moment she realized they were coming from him.

"If I bite you, we'll be able to have this conversation where no one can hear us." She looked at Shawn, who moved out of the room. "He knows you're aroused. I can smell you as well."

"I most certainly am not." He wanted to prove her wrong but only sent her a few more images before he changed the subject.

"Did you know that Carter has an office in Indiana? He's had it for about two years now. It was being funded by your estate, but I took care of that this morning." He leaned into her and heard her pulse pick up. "I want to lay you over this table and eat you."

"I wish you'd stop that." He nodded as she tried to talk about something else. "He always had a way of ending up on his feet. When I caught him in his office with a woman at his...I caught him and he had to move out of there. I wondered if he had another hidey hole."

"I think he has several. What was he doing to the woman in his office? Did he have her over the desk and you caught him fucking her? I could bend you over this table if that's what you want." Her shuddering breath told him a lot. "But the thought of eating you until you come down my throat appeals to me a great deal."

"Stop that, please?" He pulled her to him, chair and all. She didn't resist him when he picked her up and pulled her onto his lap. He had to fight hard with himself not to do just what he wanted and lay her over the table and feast on her while he adjusted her around so that she was straddled over him.

"Kiss me, Molly." She shook her head, and he moved to her neck, where her pulse was beating so quickly it was hard to see it. "I want to drink from you here. I want to taste your blood as it slides down the back of my throat. You'll come then. Tighten your pussy around my cock so that I'll have no choice but to follow you."

"You don't want me." He nipped at her throat and felt her rock over his cock. He was hard, so hard that he needed to free himself or hurt for a long time.

"I do want you. I've been thinking about you since I left you last night, and all I can think about is making you mine." He nipped harder at her throat and tasted blood. It wasn't a lot but enough to make a connection between the two of them. He pulled her over his cock again and rolled her hips up and down as he ran his free hand up her shirt to cup her breast.

"Randy, you have to stop. Anyone could see us." She didn't tell him to stop because she didn't want this, and that encouraged him. Standing up, he moved to the counter and sat her on it. Before she could protest, he pulled her shirt off over her head and then buried his face between her breasts.

"I want to suckle at your nipples." She curled her fingers into his hair, and he licked a path over the curve of her breasts as they spilled from the top of her bra. "I want to see how pink your nipples are, then make them harden for my mouth."

He pulled her bra off and stepped back to look at his bounty. They were fuller than he'd thought, and he wondered if she would go braless for him. Lifting one of the heavy orbs, he pulled her nipple into his mouth and sucked just the tip while he worked at her snap and zipper with his free hand. He had to taste her.

Her jeans came off more easily when she lifted her hips up. He reached for his own zipper when she leaned back against the cabinets, panting. As she lay before him in her panties, he could smell her. She was his, and he was going to take her. Pulling her head to his, he kissed her. His cock was so hard he knew that as soon as he entered her he was going to blow his wad. But that's not what he wanted to do. Not yet anyway. Stepping back, he nearly smiled when she whimpered.

"I'm going to feast on you." Her nod made him smile. "You're going to come down my throat, and when I've had enough, though I'm not sure that's possible, I'm going to fuck you right here and mark you with my cum."

"Please?" He grabbed the chair behind him more as something to hold him up than to sit in, but realized the advantage almost immediately. Pulling it to her, he sat down and opened her legs. Her bright yellow panties were all that was between him and his meal, and they were soaking wet.

Moving the tiny scrap of lace out of his way, Randy slipped his finger through her wet curls. The heat coming from her was enough to burn him, but he was ready for the fire. Taking his fingers to his mouth, he sucked them clean of her, moaning as he cleaned her from him. Running his hands up her thighs, he slid them under her panties and tore them from her. He spread her wide open for him and suckled her clit into his mouth. Christ, she tasted better than he ever imagined she would.

He fucked her with his tongue, filling his mouth with as much of her cream as he could. She danced over his mouth, sliding her hips up and down until he had to hold her still while he ate. Her pussy was trimmed clean, her pretty little nether lips were bare of her hair, and he found that he loved tasting her this way. As he slid his fingers into her, he heard her cry out and touched her again. Then when she cried out, his mouth was flooded with her hot juices. He drank from her as quickly as he could, not wanting to miss a single drop of her. When she pulled his head away from her, he looked at her, his wolf right on the edge.

"Fuck me." He had to think about what she was saying, and when she repeated herself to him twice more, he stood up. "Now, fuck me now. Please, Randy, fuck me."

He pulled her to the edge of the counter and moved between her legs. He freed his cock from his pants, which barely clung to his hips. Moving closer, he slid his crown over her entrance. Her pussy pulled at him, suckled at his cock, and he moved deeper, just enough to bury his crown inside of her. He didn't want to hurt her and knew that he would if he took her like he needed to. Randy should have known she wouldn't want him to be easy. She wrapped her legs around his hips and pulled his cock into her just as she took his mouth.

If he thought eating her was fantastic, fucking her was out of this world. He moved in and out of her hard and fast, knowing that with every stroke he was getting closer and closer to his own release. Pulling her hot body to his, he turned to the table where he could lay her out. Randy took her breast into his mouth as he slammed into her to the root. Molly grabbed his shoulders and clawed at him as she cried out his name. When she tilted her head, he moved his mouth over her shoulder to her throat and licked the pounding pulse. Letting his wolf go a little, he let him mark his mate as Randy came.

Her scream had him wanting more. He lifted her up even as he came and bit her again. He knew that he'd hurt her this time, but the need to make her his was taking him. As soon as she tightened around him again, he let go once more, filling her with his cum. This time he threw back his head and howled out. There wasn't a beast around that wouldn't know he'd just taken a mate.

He held her to his body as his heart started to slow. Licking the two wounds closed, he tried to tell himself that he'd not hurt her as badly as the wounds looked. Randy had never wanted to bite a woman before, even though it was part of their nature. For some reason it had always turned him off. He was glad now that he'd waited to do it with her. She was well and truly his mate. Her soft snore told him that he'd worn her out, and he lifted her up off his still hard cock to hold her.

He didn't encounter anyone as he moved through the house to the stairs. When he was at the top, he realized he had no idea where she was sleeping. Lifting his head to the air, he moved along the strongest path of her scent and found the room where the new mattress was. Someone had turned down the bed for them, and he thought about Shawn. He, too, would know that Molly was his. But she was right, the furniture in here had to go. It was...it was all Carter, and he hated it on sight.

Putting her into the bed, he stood over her as she lay there naked. Blood stained her skin where he'd bitten her, and there were a few bruises on her thighs where he'd held her a little too hard. He would have to remind himself next time that she was still human and he could and would hurt her. Reaching for his brother, he told him that he had a mate.

"About time you came around. Did she have to take you or did you finally get your head out of your ass and take her?" He told him to fuck off. *"I'm happy for you, really. Have you told Austin?"*

"Not yet." Randy sat on the other side of the bed and looked at her again. *"I think I hurt her. I forgot...she's still human."*

"She is at that." Randy felt his brother's laughter. *"I'm sure that you know this, but you have to have both hers and Austin's permission to change her. And I don't think she's going to be easy to convince."*

He didn't either and told Reid that. *"She's so...I wanted to say fragile, but that's not right either. It's like she's this wonderfully hard person who can break if I'm not careful."*

"I know what you mean. It is in our nature to want to take them hard and make them ours, but we also have to protect them. Though I'm not sure she's going to be any easier to protect than Jodie is. We have us a pair of strong-willed women." Reid laughed. *"Dad would have shit a brick if he had met them. I doubt he would have been able to bully them around like he did Mom. If one of them didn't kill him the first time they met him."*

"*Either one of them would have kicked his ass.*" Randy yawned and thought about the mess they'd made in the kitchen, and stood up to go and clean it up. But Molly shifted on the bed, and he thought about curling around her body, even for just a little bit. Crawling in beside her, he told his brother he'd talk to him later. Randy was asleep almost as soon as she wrapped around him.

CHAPTER 6

Molly woke up sore. She knew that on some level she should know why she was hurting like she'd just started training, but her mind was sort of fuzzy about it. Rolling over on the big bed, she thought about the furniture that was coming today and sat up when she realized there was someone singing in her bathroom.

"Christ, what have I done?" Randy. She'd slept with Randy. Well, sleep was something that had happened in very small doses, because they'd had sex almost all night. The sun was just coming up when she finally begged him to let her rest. His laughter made her body quake with more desire. But exhaustion won out. Molly pulled the sheet up to her breasts when the door opened from the bathroom.

He looked delicious. Well, more than that, he looked carved from a stone and maybe a little harder than it. Water dripped down his chest over the tufts of hair and to the top of the towel, which was wrapped around his hips. She had to swallow twice when she thought of what he had beneath that towel.

"You're looking at me like I'm your next meal." She nodded before she could think. "I can help you with that hunger if you want me to."

"Aren't you tired from last night? I never knew a man could go so many times and still want more." She flushed, her face heating to molten when she realized what she'd said to him. He pulled the towel off, and she licked her lips.

"Do I look like a man who's had enough?" She shook her head and watched as his thick cock grew incredibly harder as she watched. "I'm going to enjoy waking up to you every morning if you look at me like this."

"I need a shower." He continued to move toward her as he fisted his cock. "I stink and I'm pretty sure that my breath is really bad."

He kissed her and lifted his head just a little as he pulled her from the bed. "You could use a shower, but only because I want to help you wash up. Then we can make love in there until you need to come back here to rest again."

"I have things to do today." She moved ahead of him as he pushed her to the bathroom. The room was still warm from his bath, and she could smell her soap and shampoo. "I guess you'll be leaving soon after."

His laugher made her want to hit him, but he cupped her breast from behind, and she moaned. "I'm not going anywhere. But I would love to take you over this counter. When I was brushing my teeth, all I could think about was how this was the perfect height for me to fuck you this way. And I would be able to watch those lovely breasts sway back and forth as I pounded you from behind. Would you like that? I know I would."

Randy pressed her against the cool granite and bent her at the waist. His cock was at her backside, and she could already feel herself getting wet for him. When he pressed his fingers into her pussy, she spread her legs for him and felt his cock just at her entrance.

He moved into her slowly, stretching her little by little until she wanted to scream at him. When he put his hands on her hips, she felt a little twinge of pain, like he'd held her like that before, but he rolled his hips and she forgot about it. When he curled his fingers into her hair and lifted her up, she looked him in the eyes as he slowly fucked her.

"Do you know what I want to do to you right now? I want to come in your sweet pussy, then roll you over so that I can eat you again." Her body hummed with pleasure from his words. "My wolf wants to mark you. He did a little last night, but he wants to sink his canines into your flesh and make you ours."

"He wants to be a wolf while he bites me?" Randy nodded, and she could see the wolf there in his eyes. "I can see him. He's so close to your skin, I can see him race all over you."

"Can he mark you?" She watched his face as he quickened his pace. "Christ, you have no idea how much I'm having to fight him right now. He wants me to come deep inside of you so he can bite you."

"Yes. Do it. Let him bite me." Randy watched her as he stilled. When he stepped back, she turned to see him shift and it took her breath away. *"Lean on the counter. He is going to bite your thigh."*

Nodding, she sat down and moved her leg so that he could get to her thigh. His muzzle moved along her skin, and Molly moaned as his tongue laved over her. She moved when he pressed his muzzle to her inner thigh.

"He's going to lick you. I can't stop him. But he wants his taste. If you don't want this, I would suggest you hit him. Or he's going to lick you."

She found she wanted it and moved back on the counter and opened her legs. His whimper made her wet, and she closed her eyes when his hot breath burned at her pussy. Then his tongue licked her from gate to clit and she grabbed the counter harder. The second time his tongue moved over her she came, screaming out Randy's name even as he lapped at her over and over. Suddenly she was being jerked forward and Randy was there.

"I'm going to fuck you." She nodded, almost afraid of how he looked. "Christ, do you have any idea what you did to me?"

His cock filled her. There was no gentle taking this time, but he fucked her hard. He lifted her up and slammed her against the wall, and she cried out when he bit her. Her climax ripped from her so hard that she knew she'd be hoarse for a week from it. As soon as he bit her, Molly leaned forward and bit him too.

Blood filled her mouth. It was hot, spicy, like his skin tasted. She swallowed twice as his blood filled her mouth, and when she felt him lick her wound, she tried to do the same to him. But his blood flowed freely, and she licked the path of it to his nipple and suckled at him there. When he yanked her head up and kissed her with an almost savagery, she gave him as good as she got. When she came again, her body screaming through it like a tornado, she felt the darkness take her until she could only see the pin-point of light before everything went black.

~~~

"I can't wake her up." The voice rushed through his mind so quickly and so full of panic that Austin had no

idea who it was. *"You have to come here. I think I've killed her and I can't wake her up. Fuck, Austin, I never thought it would be like this with her, and now I've killed her."*

"Randy?" He told him yes and started to babble again. *"Calm down and tell me what happened. And if you have killed your mate, it will be the first time in history. Just take a deep breath and tell me what you did."*

"I...we were having sex." That much Austin had figured out. He'd been in the same panicky situation when he and CJ had had some pretty intense sex before she'd been changed. *"I never meant to hurt her, but she let him taste her."*

"Who?" Austin knew what he was going to say before he told him and nearly burst out laughing.

"My wolf. All he wanted to do was mark her, and she said it was okay, but she, well she gave him more and he liked it. But I did, too, and when I took her, I didn't remember she was human and I killed her." Austin reached for CJ and told her he had to make a run to Molly's house. She said she was going too. *"Are you there? What do I do? I can't...I didn't want to live with her, and now I don't know what I'll do without her."*

"Shut the fuck up and stop saying you killed her. Is she fucking breathing?" He hated to talk to the young man this way, but he had to snap him out of his panic. *"And put your fingers over her pulse. Is there one?"*

"I can see her chest moving up and down, and her pulse? It's really fast. Is she having a heart attack?" Austin did laugh then. *"I don't think this is the least bit funny. I've never bitten anyone before."*

That brought him up short. *"Never? You've never bitten a woman during sex? Ever? Why not?"*

"I don't know why not. It just didn't feel right." He could feel the younger man's embarrassment and felt badly for it. *"She's the first, and it's only right that she should be. My dad used to bite people. He would tear into our skin when he was*

really pissed. Then he'd sit back and laugh while he didn't let us shift to heal. I was never going to be that way."

Austin wanted to find the bastard that had been their sire and kill him all over. The few times he'd talked to their father he'd wanted to kill him then. The boys had told him when he'd found them that their parents were dead. It had taken him almost a month of them living with him and CJ to find out they had thrown their children out in favor of keeping their welfare money.

"I'll be there in a few minutes. Just keep her warm, and if you haven't already, get dressed. I'm not in the mood to see your naked ass when I get there." Austin moved out of his office and toward the living room when he felt Randy touch his mind again.

"Austin, I know that I'm nearly too old for this and you might not want me to, but I'd very much like to tell you that you were a better father to me than most would have been. You've never been anything but there for me, more than anyone ever was before. And I love you like I never loved my own father." There was a pause where Austin had to hold onto the wall or be felled by what this young man had said. *"I love you very much."*

The connection was cut off, but Austin could feel his love as he was bathed in it. He wasn't sure he could feel any better than he did at that moment. He found CJ coming toward him and pulled her into his arms, baby and all.

"He loves me." She looked up at him confused. "Randy. He just told me that I was like a father to him and that he loved me. I've always known that he and Reid loved me. I just never thought it would feel this fucking fantastic when they said it to me. I'm so overwhelmed that I want to jump for joy."

CJ held him to her as he basked in the joy. He looked down at her and realized that while he might have been the father figure in the boy's life, CJ had been more of a mother than anything. He started to tell her that when she spoke first.

"He's called me 'mom' a few times. But I'm not sure…I never said anything about it, but I know how you feel. It's like you've been given a gift and you just don't know how to process it." He nodded over her head and pulled his little girl into his arms. She, too, was a gift, and when she smiled at him with her beautiful mouth, he thought of Molly.

"I think he's changed her. I don't know that for sure, but I can tell that something's happened to her." He moved back enough to snuggle with his daughter as he continued. "Anyone tries to have sex with my daughters is going to die. I'm just putting that out there so that when I have to go to prison for killing a man, you'll know that I did warn you about it. No one is touching any of my children, especially my daughters."

CJ laughed, but he was serious. He knew what men were like, especially men who were wolves. If anyone even came near one of his kids, even if they just happened to be their mates, it was going to be game over and bury them in the back yard. He was never going to have to go through this with one of his own kids.

CJ punched him in the arm, and he looked at her. He could tell that she didn't believe him. And that was fine by him. He knew she'd be pissy about it, and he wasn't in the mood to argue with her today. Besides, he knew that he'd lose anyway and he wasn't ready for that either. CJ could make him whimper more than any person could, and it didn't have to do with just her sexual nature. She was a she-wolf of the rarest kind. They both went out to the car, and he looked around the yard while she buckled Aerial into her seat. His mother came out when he was just about to get into the vehicle.

"I'd like to go over there, too." She nodded to him as if he'd okayed it. Not that he'd deny her anything, but he did notice that she had her spoon in her hand. She looked at it when he did. "I might find a need to use it. You never know."

"I do know, and you will. What makes you think that Randy has messed...?" He thought about what he was going to say and shook his head. "Never mind. I might need it myself. He's hurt her somehow, and he's scared out of his mind about it. He's been screaming at me that he's killed her for the past ten minutes. Maybe you can knock some sense into his empty head for me."

"He didn't hurt her, and we both know it. I've never seen a boy so set on making things hard for himself. I bet you dollars to donuts that he wants her to sell that house thinking that he can't afford to pay for it. What I read, that little girl has more money than you do."

Austin knew she did. After the will was read he'd talked to Phil and he'd told him that with her money and property alone she was worth billions. And then there was the insurance policies as well as all the jewelry. The sister had invested well and had not been an idiot with her money. And once Randy's money was put with it, they'd be able to do whatever they wanted forever.

"Are you going to have a serious talk with that boy?" He looked at his mother in the rearview mirror when she spoke. "About helping you out as an alpha. You know as well as I do that boy has the temperament for it. I'm surprised you haven't done it before now. You sure have blustered about it enough."

Austin laughed. "Mom, you do know that the *boy* is twenty-seven years old, don't you? I don't think he'll like you calling him that now that he has himself a mate."

"Like he's going to be any older than me. I think he enjoys me calling him that. Makes him think I love him or something." Austin looked at her again, and she smiled. "Yes, son, I love him. He's like a son to me. Both of them are. I just wished...someday I wish I had more time."

Austin felt his heart take a twist. He knew that she was getting up there in years and thanks to Phil, who had given her a little of the gift he had, she'd been around longer than she would have been under normal circumstances. But he could see she was getting tired. And he had to stop and think that his mom was over seventy years old. He didn't want to think about her leaving him.

"Mom, are you happy?" She looked at him, then at CJ before she nodded. "You would tell me if you needed anything, right?"

"Whatever would I need?" She huffed at him. "Of all the things to say to me. I have more grandchildren than most people. I have eight of the best sons in the world, friends that would and have given me more love than some children do. And the best of all, I have you right here where I can see you every day if I want. What a thing to say. Do I need anything? What would I need, I ask you again?"

Austin glanced at CJ and saw her fighting tears. He hadn't meant to make any of them upset, but he didn't want to lose any of them either. He pulled into the drive and turned to look at his mom.

"I love you more than I thought possible. And even though over the years I've wanted to burn your spoon, it holds the fondest memories a man could have." She hit him between the eyes with the spoon so fast he had to blink several times before he could speak. "What the hell was that for?"

She opened the door and started out before she looked at him with a smile. "I'm just creating memories for you. You do like memories, don't you son? You wouldn't want to deny your poor old mother giving you memories before she dies, would you?"

When she shut the door and made her way to the house, he looked at CJ as she sat beside him. She was laughing so hard she was wiping at tears. Austin didn't understand women and doubted he ever would. Getting out, he went around the car to get his daughter and leaned down to whisper in her ear.

"You should know that when she's gone I'm going to burn that thing." He kissed her cheek and went up to the house still talking to Aerial. "Come on little girl, let's see what the poor boy has gotten himself into now."

Shawn was waiting for him when he entered. Austin had no idea why but he'd never really trusted the older panther. But his wife had been giving him treats since he'd been a little kid. It was funny how things moved around so that you met in the middle more often than not. He handed over Aerial when he asked for her but wondered if she'd be all right. Aerial looked at him as if to say, "I've got this, Dad." And that was another thing he'd never really cared for about the man, his lack of a smile. Ever. Aerial toddled after Shawn, holding his finger and looking up at him like she was slightly leery of him, yet, like a baby, still wasn't sure why. Austin decided that he'd have the man investigated as soon as he got back to his house. Austin went to the study where he heard voices.

"I do not have to see your brother. I'm perfectly fine." Austin looked at Molly when she got up to pace and thought she looked great but said nothing. "Are you going to be this way if I get shot again? And I'm pretty sure I will. Or I might just shoot you."

"Are you planning on getting shot again?" Austin was wondering the same thing when his mom asked her. "If you do then would you mind not telling me until you're healed up? That way I can beat your ass and not have to worry about it hurting you more. I've never met a woman more bent on...well, that's not true. All the women in this family seemed to have a flair for getting hurt one way or another."

Molly huffed before she spoke. "I'm a big girl and I'm pretty sure I can take care of myself. And no, I'm not planning on getting shot, but it is part of the job. And before I forget, Martin is coming over. He's going to the...we're going out to the...." Austin knew what she was trying her best not to say. She was going out to where it had happened, where she and her sister had been shot.

"I'll go with you." They all stared at Jodie who walked in the room. "I might be able to see stuff you won't. Also, congratulations are in order I guess."

The flush on Molly's face was funny, but he wisely kept his laughter to himself. He looked at Randy, who was sitting there like he was waiting for the hammer to drop or something. He'd not moved or said anything since he'd come into the room. Austin went to sit next to him.

"I guess you didn't kill her." He looked at him, and Austin could see the fear in his eyes. "I'm not mad. I'm not even surprised. Are you okay with changing her?"

"I don't know…it's like…she's my mate and I've only just realized that I love her. And I could have killed her." Austin started shaking his head when his mom came to sit on the other side of Randy. "She could have died when I bit her. What the hell was I thinking?"

Bam! The spoon was out and whacking Randy in the head quickly. Randy looked at his mom as he rubbed his head. She looked ready to do battle. Austin decided this had less to do with memories and more to do with her making her point stick. He was pretty sure it would too.

"What were you thinking when you changed her? Having her in your life for the rest of your days? Or were you just thinking she was a good lay?" Randy flushed darker and closed his mouth tight. "I know what you were thinking. You were thinking you'd get us all over here and let your mate suffer through this on her own. Look at her."

They both did, and Austin could see the fear in her eyes, too. She was not just afraid but terrified. He heard his mom ask Randy what he'd told her about her being a wolf.

"I didn't say anything to her. She woke up about ten minutes after I talked to Austin and then she came down here. I told her we needed to talk, but she kept talking about getting her sister's murderer taken care of. I don't even know if she knows that she's a wolf now."

"She knows. But since you've been worried about Austin beating you for not asking for permission, she's been worried that you feel you've made a mistake." Randy looked at him, then at his mom. "You know that you have to ask permission, but not one of my sons ever did. And even if they had, it was too late. The girls in this

92

family are here to stay. Go to her, boy, and tell her you love her."

Randy stood, then sat down. When he stood the second time, his mom gave him a little push. He went to Molly and pulled her into his arms, and she looked ready to crumble as he held her upright. Austin had a feeling the girl was barely hanging on, and this would break her. She looked up at Randy, and even from across the room he could see the relief in her face.

"Everyone," Randy said to the room while never taking his eyes off Molly. "I'd like you all to meet my mate. We're going to get married as soon as it can be arranged, if she'll have me, and also, she's my wolf. And I've never been happier than I am right now in my entire life."

He kissed her then, and Austin looked at his mom. "How do you do that? How do you know just what to say to make things perfect?"

"I'm a mom." He waited for more, but she stood up and went to the couple. As far as Austin was concerned, that didn't explain anything. But he did get up and congratulate the couple, too. This was the oddest start to a morning he'd ever had.

When Martin and Dallas showed up a few minutes later, Shawn announced lunch. He moved out of the room as if he expected them all to follow. Aerial came into the room, and he leaned down and picked her up in his arms. He thought it odd for just a few seconds that she didn't smell like the panther at all. When as one they moved out of the office toward the door, Austin stopped and looked at the board leaning on a chair. It was finished.

"Christ." He looked at Tristian when he appeared beside him, his voice full of awe. He had to agree, Randy did a better job than he'd thought he would when Tristian asked him if he could work on it. The way it was lined up and color-coded, it looked like he might have spent days on it working nonstop.

"I didn't do it." He looked at Randy when he spoke. "Well, I helped, but Molly did the most of it. She said it was driving her crazy and she needed it finished. I think she really enjoyed doing it. And once she explained to me how she was working it, it sort of flew together. She has a great mind, and I loved watching her make this work for us."

"She does, and I knew that you'd be good at this sort of thing too. But that makes me think that I need to talk to you about something now rather than later." Austin looked at the board, knowing that he'd have her do the same to his bylaws when things settled. "I need a partner. Another alpha, and I'd like for it to be you."

"No, you should ask your brothers." Randy started away, then stopped. "I'm honored, but I really don't think I'm the man for the job. I'm young, and we both know that they'll never accept me as much as they would one of your brothers."

"I disagree. And my brothers, all of them, agreed you'd be the man for the job. They all said that they'd follow you quicker than they would anyone else they knew. And your law degree will help you with the humans, and with you being a part of my family, you know how I like things run. You could do things your way to a degree, but I truly think you and I would work very well together."

"You're serious." Austin nodded and Tristian patted him on the back. "I don't know what to say. I'm...well, I just don't know what to say. I'd have to talk it over with Molly, of course."

"Talk what over with Molly?" Molly walked into the room as she asked. "Actually, you can tell me over lunch. I'm not holding it up because you guys are in here bonding or something. I'm starved and you'll be shit out of luck if you don't get in there soon. Dallas is filling his plate again already."

He followed them into the dining room and stopped. Christ, this room was bigger than his living room and kitchen combined. Austin looked at Dallas and could see his mind working too. They had to have the next council meeting here. There was plenty of room and nobody would have to share a seat. Now he had to work on Randy being his second alpha. The house and room alone would be nice, but the man could help him more than he knew.

Austin sat down at the table and was passed several platters at once. He also noticed that more food was being brought from the room beyond, and wondered how long they'd been cooking. As soon as he bit into his steak, he moaned. Oh yeah, he thought. This was the way to have a luncheon.

CHAPTER 7

The ground looked no different than the other surrounding area. Molly got down on her knees and ran her hand over the grass, and thought about the blood that had been left there. Her sister was gone, and she was no closer to finding the one who did this than she'd been the day it happened. She knew from the reports that Carter hadn't shot them, but she knew as surely as she was sitting there that he'd had something to do with it.

"The shooter came from the west, you told me." She looked up at Martin, who had shown up just as they were finishing lunch. He'd been made a plate of food, and she'd made him sit as she went over the files he'd brought her. "You said five shots, but according to the doc, you guys had been shot seven times total."

"I didn't hear them, I guess, but yeah, the shots came from that way." She looked at the grass again and closed her eyes. "There was no time between the impact and the sound. So since a bullet can travel at about 1,865 feet per second, and times about 1,100, that means he was within a thousand feet of us. It had to be that close or I would never have heard it."

She stood up, and they started west. Molly tried to think who would be good enough to fire from that range and not miss his target. Reid and Randy came up to walk on either side of them, and Martin explained what they were doing as she led the way.

"We're going to have a look at the area the shots might have come from. Probably nothing there, but we gotta try. Could be he left a casing or a butt of something. Don't know if the shooter was a smoker, but we'll never know unless we have a look-see." Randy took her hand, and she let him. Her body seemed to hum with something, and she wasn't sure how to ask about it without feeling stupid.

"It's your wolf. She wants to come out and help you. She can feel your stress." She looked at Reid when he spoke. His wink embarrassed her for some reason. "You'll get the hang of it."

"We'll go out and play when we get back to your house." She looked at Randy and wondered if he knew that he kept calling it her house. It was her sister's house, not hers. She was only staying there because...well, because. When Randy spoke again, she felt him in her mind and nearly stumbled.

"*Careful. And you should know that if you reach out, you can read other people's thoughts too. I had it given to me by Jodie, and she assures me that you have it as well.*" There was no way she was going to look into other people's heads. His laughter made her realize he was listening to her. "*You might be surprised to know that you can learn a great deal about someone if you do it right. Like your boss there, he's wondering if now that he's retired, Austin will put him out to pasture or let him work on projects like some old feeble person. I think he'll be a good addition to our security team. He's got a good head on his shoulders.*"

"You think he'd do that? Austin, I mean, do you think he'd do that to my friend?" She looked at Martin, just realizing how old he looked. *"I didn't know he was a wolf until your brother told me. How is it he could work in the department and no one noticed?"*

"The same way your butler and his wife worked with your sister and she never noticed." She nodded. *"Also, you have a were tiger as well as a bear working for you and — "*

"Okay. First of all, it's not my house. If anything, it's my sister's. And failing that, it's got to be our house. I'm not the only one living there, and won't be so long as we can be together. Unless, of course, you're wanting to get rid of me. But then, why the fuck did you change me if you were? If that's the case, I'm going to murder you in your sleep. If you ever sleep. I haven't had a full night of rest since I met you and you had sex with me." She realized she was shouting out loud when someone behind her laughed. Turning, she looked at Reid and saw that Martin had moved ahead of them. "You think this is funny? I don't. I'm living in a house that I should hate but can't because I can see my sister in there. I have more money than I've...hell, I've never in my life dreamt I'd have any, and now I have too much. I'm a wolf mated to a lawyer, and I have no job and no prospect of finding one until I can get this settled. And let's not forget that I have a man out gunning for me. Did I miss anything?"

"Nope, I think you pretty much covered it. But you should know several things right off. The house belongs to you and Randy. If you don't want it, sell it. If it makes you happy, then by all means keep it. You can certainly afford to. And that brings me to the money. You're a good deal richer than you thought. I don't know if Randy's had a chance to tell you yet, but he's worth millions himself. Not like you, but he could support you if you wanted to walk away from what your sister wanted you to have. You have a lawyer for a mate. Good for you. It might make you think twice before you turn to a life of crime, or you could be really good at it knowing all the laws. As for you having a job? Not a problem either. You don't need to work, so you can hold out for anything you want." Reid winked at her again. He did that a lot, she thought. "As for you reading people's minds? You should search the mind of your brother-in-law while you're getting used to the way to do things. It might help you in figuring out who he hired."

"Fuck me." She looked around and then at Randy. "This mind reading thing? Does it apply to everything or just people?"

He looked over her shoulder, and she knew he was asking Reid. Then he looked back with a nod. "Anything you touch will give you some feedback. What did you have in mind?"

She took off running in the direction that Martin went. She looked back to where Austin and Dallas were standing where they'd been shot, and figured it was about nine hundred feet. Taking off her boots and socks, she dug her toes in the ground and moved around when she didn't get anything. She did this several times until she knew where the man stood. Smiling, she leaned down and dug around in the dirt until she found what she was looking for. Without touching it, she asked for a baggie, and Martin handed her one. She held up the wad of gum and looked at Randy.

"We have DNA." Martin looked around the area, and so did she. If there was gum, then there might be more. She dug deeper in the ground and laughed when both Randy and Reid did the same.

"I might have to steal this idea when Jodie and I are out on a hunt." She nodded, not really sure what they did for a living other than him being a doctor. Randy leaned over and pulled a small ring out of the dirt. It looked as if it might have been there for a very long time, so they kept looking.

They found more than they needed. Some old coins that Martin said he'd look into, some jewelry that she thought was old but really didn't know, and a shell casing. It wasn't from the high-powered rifle that she'd been told had been used, but they kept it anyway and marked it as evidence. They were moving back to where she had been hurt when she felt something stir in the air. She looked up when she saw a beautiful bird fly over and then land near Reid. When she shifted, Molly took a step back from Jodie.

"I'm sorry. I thought you knew." Molly shook her head as Randy took her hand. "I'm a shifter with a little more. I can take the form of anything and anyone. Even you."

The shift from Jodie to herself was amazing. Even her clothes were the same. Molly took a step back when Jodie took one toward her. It was just too freaky.

"I guess you could do a lot of damage to someone if they thought...." She looked at Randy. "He could think she was still alive. My sister...she could freak him out a little if he thought she was still hanging around."

"I don't understand." Then the light seemed to go off. "Holy Christ, we could haunt him. Make him think that he failed all the way around."

"And what would you gain from this?" Martin looked at the group of them and started to nod his head. "If you did it right, went to him with all this spit and fire, you could scare him enough that he'd give it up before he could think. I'm assuming you're talking about the shooter?"

"No, I'm thinking we get the shooter from the back door. Go and see Carter, scare him into calling the man he hired, and then we nail both their asses. I don't know if he would actually know the shooter. And even if he did, it might not be his real name." Molly felt her mind working out all the details as she made her way back to the house. "I don't know how to do this changing stuff, but I could learn. Then go in and tell him what a bastard I think he is for trying to kill me and —" Someone touched her arm and before she could think about who it might have been, she flipped them over and onto the ground. Her gun was at their chin before she blinked away her instinct.

"You didn't even think, did you?" Molly looked down at Jodie and shook her head, thinking the woman was going to kill her. "Nah, I'm impressed. You took me down like I was nothing. I love it. When you and Randy take the alpha job, you can be his enforcer. It will scare the shit out of those bad-assed males."

She looked up at Randy when he cleared his throat. "I never said I'd take the job. I'm not even sure it's a good idea that I even think about it. We just got mated, and what if Austin decides that someone else is more suited for the job?"

"What alpha job?" Molly got off Jodie and helped her up. She looked at Austin when Randy didn't answer her. "You thinking of quitting, old man? I understand from most of the people I've talked to that you're the shit when it comes to ruling people. Not that you're going to rule me, but you're supposed to be really good at it. Are you thinking of quitting while you can still get around without a walker?"

Nancy laughed but moved toward the house without saying anything. She'd met them in the yard a few minutes ago. Molly had heard about her, too, and also her lethal spoon. One of the brothers—she thought it was Connor—had said that it was worse than a gun and just as painful to be hit by it. She looked at them when she realized no one was answering. She glared at Austin.

"I offered him a job, and he said he'd talk to you about it before he accepted." Austin looked at Randy, then back at her as he continued to explain. "I'm more sure now than I was before he could help me out. It would be a huge responsibility, but you'd get a lot in return."

"I don't need any more money." He nodded, and then she turned to Randy. "You should do it. You'd be very good at it. And I know a great many people look up to you. Most of the people I have talked to said you were going to represent them if they needed help."

"Yeah, I'm thinking my plate will be full for a while." Randy took her hand and slowed them down so that the others could get well ahead of them before he told her what he was thinking. "I want the job, but we'd have to work together on it. And since you've...we've made no decisions on the house or the money, I thought I'd wait to see what you wanted...we wanted to do."

"Do you like living here? I don't mean in the neighborhood, but this house." She looked at the house and fell in love with it all over. She was getting over the fact that Mary didn't like the house because Carter had lived there with her. But he'd be in prison soon and they'd have nothing more to worry about concerning him. "I love that I can go into certain rooms and find bits of her there.

And some of the memories you and I are making are wonderful too."

"I want the house. I know it's really huge, but if we take this alpha job, we're going to need something big. Not to mention when we have children, we want them to have as much room as possible to grow."

"Children? Let's not get ahead of ourselves here. I don't even know how to hold one, much less raise one." He pulled her to him for a kiss. "What was that for?"

"You didn't say no. The rest is easy from here." She didn't know how he'd gotten to that conclusion but moved toward the house with him. She saw Shawn and went to him when he motioned for her to come to him.

"Miss? Will the family be staying for dinner as well?" She looked at the room now overflowing with adults and children. Where the hell had they all come from? "If so, might I suggest that we bring in more help? I will not be able to serve them all with just the staff we have now."

Molly put her fingers in her mouth and let out a shrill whistle. Everyone in the room froze in mid-step. Even the babies stopped and looked at her. This was kinda cool, and she thought she'd remember this the next time they all got together.

"Who's staying for dinner?" Everyone raised their hands, and Austin raised both his. "Okay. I'm thinking...steaks, potatoes, and maybe, I don't know, burgers for the kids?"

"I'll make a pie or two if there's room in the kitchen." Shawn nodded at Mrs. Force, and she went around him to the kitchen. They both grinned when they heard her say "Oh my" as she entered.

"You'll need to call in some pack." Molly looked at Randy, who nodded at Austin's suggestion. "And call the grocer. They'll be able to bring you supplies that come from our pantry until you get your own set up. You're entitled to use it if you run low so long as you contribute it when the monthly shopping comes around. Mom can set you up the account to use for your pack."

Molly was passing out some pads of paper and pens for notes when she realized what Austin had said. She looked over at Randy, and he smiled. Okay, he got it and was okay. So she guessed they were now alphas. Molly needed to set up some time to talk to CJ. That woman knew everything.

~~~

Randy looked around the groaning table. They were all here and working hard to bring justice for the death of Mary Ravenhall. He'd never been more proud in his entire life. When he turned to one of the children who was tugging on his arm, he smiled down at little Gordon. He was the cutest kid he'd seen, and he started to pick him up when he spoke.

"You think that lady is ever gonna pick me up?" Randy looked at where he was pointing and saw that he meant Molly. "She sure has a lot of excuses why I can't be sitting on her lap. And her being a wolf and all. Don't she get it that we like to cuddle? I don't like it as much as some of the girls do, but I can get used to it. She sure is pretty, huh?"

"She's never held a kid before." Gordon looked at him with total disbelief and could see the kid was falling in love with his mate too. "I'm not kidding. She told me today that she had no idea about kids and babies. I think she's more afraid of that than all the bad guys in the world. Do you think you can help me out with this?"

"That's a lot of bad guys, Uncle Randy. A whole lot of them." Gordon looked at his little sister, then at him. "You think she'd hold little Daisy? I'll make sure she don't drop her or nothing. I bet that would make her not scared anymore. My Daisy is the best sister in the world."

Gordon loved his little sister more than he did ice cream, he'd told him once. He also told him she didn't stink, especially after his mom put that butt powder all over her. When Randy nodded, Gordon went to his dad and pulled him down to talk to him. Randy nearly burst out laughing when Gordon was handed his seven-month-old sister, and then he took her to Molly.

"Oh kid, I don't think so. She might scream or something." Gordon shoved his sister at her again, and when her fingers touched Daisy, he took a step back. She'd either hold her or drop her. Thankfully, she held the little girl.

To say who was more confused would have been a toss-up. Daisy looked at Molly, and she right back at her. Of course, she was holding the baby under her arms and as far from her body as she could. When Daisy started to pucker her lower lip in what no doubt would have been a monstrous wail, Molly looked at Randy.

"Fix her." He moved closer to her but didn't take the baby when she tried to shove her back at him. "She's going to scream, and that will piss them off. And I'll get pissy, too, because I'll feel stupid. You so don't want me to feel stupid. I get nasty."

"Hold her better and she won't need fixing." Molly tried again to give Daisy to him, but he showed her how to hold her. "She likes to look around. Just set her on your knee and wrap your hands around her waist like this."

Molly perched the baby on her knee and wrapped her arms around her like she was a football. After a few more lessons, Daisy turned to look at Molly as if to say, "It's about fucking time." And once she realized that the woman who held her wasn't going to hurt her, she turned to the room and began jabbering again. Within minutes, the other kids, with Gordon as their leader, came to stand next to Randy and ask more questions than he thought possible. And Molly answered them all. A few of them had him thinking Molly might need a lesson or two in how much was too much concerning children, but they hung on her every word like it was gospel. And after another hour, she was letting them take turns sitting with her in the big chair. He moved away from her when his chair was commandeered.

It was nearing midnight when they all left. Reid and Jodie had stayed over; their little boy had fallen asleep on one of the beds in the upstairs bedrooms. A girl from the pack had volunteered to watch him there. Randy yawned and stretched out before the fireplace as Reid and Jodie sat in an overstuffed chair. Molly was leaning against the opposite side of the couch that he was on so he pulled her feet to his lap.

"So, you're a new alpha." Randy nodded but didn't commit. He and Molly still had to talk about it. Not just that but with everything that was going on, money was going to be a big topic, he thought. "About this thing we're doing tomorrow, you think it's a good plan?"

"I do." Molly answered before he did. "The DNA will be a few more days to come back, and we might find out it's from some kid out looking for mushrooms. I'm not sure Carter will be stupid enough to give us a name, but with you guys there, you can get something from him."

The plan was for them to go in as a group. Jodie was going to be Mary and move around the office and the area surrounding the building where Carter was holed up to scare him shitless. Then she was going to go in and make tar-tar of his ass. Not really, but she was going to make the man sit up and take notice. They'd even downloaded a map of the building he was in so they could have a few wolves there in the event that something went wrong. Not that any of them thought it would, but Randy had insisted on it.

The few times Jodie shifted to her sister, he'd had to hold onto Molly. The pain was great, but she said that Jodie had it right. And the few more times she'd shifted, to get her used to seeing her sister, the better she'd been at handling it. But Randy was still worried for her.

"Your sister and brother-in-law? Why did they marry in the first place, do you know? I mean, no offense, but your sister could have done a good deal better than that slimy shit." Jodie looked at Molly when she realized what she'd said. "I'm so sorry. Sometimes I don't think before I speak."

"It's okay. I know what you meant. And she could have, but he'd blackmailed her. I didn't know it at the time, but he'd told her that if he went to the police and told them what had really happened that night was that I'd killed that girl, then I'd lose my scholarship and be out on my ass. I didn't of course, but instead of coming to me with the threat, she married him. I don't think he was ever planning to stay with her, but when she started making it big, he hung around for the money." Molly wiped at her face, and Randy could feel her sorrow. "I miss her more and more every day. She really thought she was saving me, but I couldn't save her when she needed me most."

"You did too." They all looked at Reid when he spoke. "You saved her every time you came to see her. And why do you think she filed for divorce in the first place? It wasn't because she'd suddenly had enough. It was because you told her you were there for her. And you were. From what Phil told me, when she came to his office she was more terrified of disappointing you than what Carter would do to her. She didn't want that from you. But you have to explain about that night. What happened?"

"He killed a girl. In a drunken rage, I guess you could say. Mary wouldn't go out with him and he was pissed. We started to walk home, but he wasn't having it. The story he told said that he'd gotten out of the car and it slipped out of park." She shook her head. "He never put it into park. As soon as he was clear of it, it started to roll. And he'd knocked Sandra Middleton, a girl that Mary went to school with, in the path of it. He crushed her head with the car and then told the police that stupid story about her falling." Molly got up to pace. "The next morning before I left for college again, I went to see his coach. Carter was this big shit football player and had all kinds of people wanting him to sign with him. It's where the car came from. But the coach told me to fuck off basically and that if it got out that he'd been drinking as well as the girl was murdered and not involved in an accident, then the whole school would suffer. So I headed to the bigger paper across town. The one in the opposing team as a matter of fact. The shit hit the fan, and he lost it all."

"You did that?" She nodded at Reid, and he laughed. "Good for you! Christ, I wish I had been there. I would love to have seen his face when he found out he was getting nothing. Must have been a big hole put in his ego."

"He got his revenge, I guess." Randy pulled her to him when he felt her pain again. "I guess he won in the long run. My sister is dead, and he's still out there living it up. If this doesn't work and we can't convict him, I don't know what I'll do. It's such a nightmare. I'd gone to see Carter after Mary told me what he'd done. I can't help but think he might not have killed her had I just held my tongue. But he'd pissed me off. The fucking bastard was taking everything from her, including her happiness. I hated him for that."

"Well of course you did. The fucking prick is going to get his payback or I'll kill him myself." Randy looked at Jodie to see if she might be kidding. And when he wasn't sure, he looked at Reid. His shrug was not helpful at all.

After another hour, they all went up to bed. Randy thought about staying down and talking to Reid a little more, but Molly looked so sad that he went up with her. As soon as he got into bed with her, she rolled over into his arms and cried herself to sleep.

It was the longest and most painful night of his life.

CHAPTER 8

Carter was looking over his lack of finances when someone knocked on the door. He looked up when the door opened without his permission and was startled to see his secretary being held at gunpoint by none other than Molly Barker.

"You should know that when you let her go, I'm going to have you arrested." Molly snorted at him but didn't move. "Let her go and let's talk about what you're going to give me or I'll have you brought up on charges."

"I'm not worried about you. You know as well as I do that whatever you think you have against me, it's nothing compared to the hurt I'm going to bring down on you when I can prove you killed my sister." Carter started to reach under his desk for the gun, but something poked him in the head. "I'd like you to meet my lawyer, Phil Campbell. I understand you've been looking for us."

That fucking idiot he had sent to bring Molly and Phil to his office had been arrested yesterday. Trespassing of all things. And then they'd found his car. Carter had no idea what the fool thought he was going to do with enough firepower to take on a small country, but now he was in jail awaiting a hearing. As far as Carter was concerned, he could rot there. He looked at Molly when he saw a movement and felt his body freeze again. There she was again.

"Do you see that?" Before he finished the question, Mary was gone again. Carter was having hallucinations, and now they had followed him to his work. "She was right there."

The first time he'd seen Mary, he'd been standing in his bathroom shaving. The hotel had shitty service, but he knew this was only temporary and had overlooked the cheap faucets and non-heated floors. He was going to get his house back if it was the last thing he did. But the image of Mary standing behind him had him cutting his face as he jerked around.

The second time he'd seen her, he'd been in his limo. Carter really didn't have a lot of things to look up on his computer on the way to his job, so he'd been playing a game. But again a movement caught his eye. This time she spoke.

"Hello, asshole. How are you getting along without my money?" He nearly wet himself when she suddenly disappeared. Carter sat there until his car came to a stop. Then he nearly leapt from the car. And now this.

"See what?" Molly smiled at him and for whatever reason, he thought she knew what he was seeing. She moved toward his desk and helped his secretary sit down. "Alice tells me that you're planning a big raid on my house. It seems you've hidden things everywhere on the estate and plan to go back and get it."

"Who?" He had no idea who this Alice person was, and Carter was equally sure she'd had a camera in his office. There was no way she had this plan that well versed. "I want you to leave here right now."

"She's this woman here. She's been working for you for years, you idiot." Carter looked at the woman in the chair, and she nodded. Christ, how the hell was he supposed to know all the people who worked for him? The man still holding a gun to his head laughed before he spoke.

"You're so fucked. You know that, right? A man who gives away secrets during pillow talk can't have all that long to live." Carter stood up to turn on him, completely forgetting the gun for a few seconds. It smacked him hard between the eyes, and he sat back down. "Move again and I'll shoot you because I can."

"I never slept with her. I don't care that much about sex to go around fucking women that are beneath me." He looked at Alice and smiled. "Tell them that we've never had sex and I'll get you out of this."

He was going to kill her was what he was going to do. Just as soon as he was free he was going to wrap his fingers around her fucking neck and squeeze the life out of her. He had no idea how she knew what he was going to do, but Molly had too much information not to have gotten it from someone. Carter started to speak when he saw Mary again. This time she looked as she had when he'd gone to the coroner's office to identify her body.

"You should know that I'm going to haunt you forever, Carter. And when you're dead and in your own hell, I'm going to continue to haunt you because you're a lying son of a bitch and I hate you." Carter felt his heart take a hit, like he'd been stabbed there, and put his hand out to grab for his meds. But the man behind him knocked them away. "You really don't expect anyone to help you, do you? I mean, what did you ever do for me but make my life a living hell?"

"You had a good life despite the hurt I'd put on you. And I quit hitting you in the face when you lost that big part. How the hell...? You should know better than to piss me off. We've had this conversation enough for you to get it by now." Carter looked at Molly and Alice. "My dear wife is threatening me. She seems to think that I'm going to be haunted by her for the rest of my days."

"Mr. Ravenhall, you do know that your wife is dead, don't you?" Carter snarled at Alice when she spoke. But when Mary moved behind her and put her fingers on her head, Alice looked around, but Mary had already disappeared.

"She's been popping in and out all day. She was even in the bathroom with me this morning." He felt a burble of laughter bubble up, and he had to fight hard to swallow it. He wasn't going to have them think he was insane. If they did, they'd have grounds to have him committed. Then he couldn't kill Molly and now it seemed Mary from a padded cell. "I think she's trying to have me admit something that will get me into trouble."

"Do you have something to admit?" He looked at Molly and wondered if she really thought he'd answer that. "You killed her and tried to have me killed too. Why? She was your ticket to a better life."

"If it were true that I had something to do with her death and you being hurt, what do you think might have happened had she divorced me? And you kept egging her on and on, didn't you? Do you supposed you might have been the cause of her death?"

He knew he'd hit a nerve but had little time to relish the fact. The man behind him put him in a world of hurt as he did something that made him slam his head twice on the desk. When Carter could see again, he noticed that any pain he might have caused Molly was covered up now by hatred. Christ, he'd never realized before how beautiful she really was.

"You'll answer my questions, not make up shit on your own." He hit the table again just as Molly finished speaking. "Tell me who you hired to shoot us and I might let you live for another day."

"You mean the rule follower Molly Barker is now going to be the bad guy? Oh no, say it isn't so." Mary appeared behind her again, and he looked right at her this time. "You fucking cunt. All you had to do was leave me the fuck alone and let me spend all that money when I wanted to. What the hell were you going to do with it? You never spent a fucking dime on anyone, not even yourself. And that house? I hope to Christ no one ever finds the shit I have hidden all over it. It would be just what you deserve."

"Oh but I have found it." He looked at her hard, trying to figure out if she was bullshitting him. "The money in the safe in the floor of your bedroom? Then there was the wall safe you had put in behind the bookshelves in my office. I also have found the money you had hidden in my studio. You just couldn't let me have any space of my own, could you? You had to go in and rearrange things to suit what you had thought of as a queen of the big screen."

"You lie." The small safe hit his desk with a loud thud. He started to reach for it but looked up to see Alice looking as his spectra. "You see her? Do you see my wife?"

"I'm not sure." The woman looked at him, and Carter had a moment of profound terror. She looked...the wolf staring back at him made his bladder loosen just enough to have him feel a dampness cover his thigh. "You should have been a better husband. Do you know what she's going to do to you now? Your ex-wife and her sister are going to make you pay."

The wolf changed again into a man. Then he was his wife, then a panther. Carter wet himself. Fear made his mind close down and he had no idea what to do now. Looking up at the man who still held the gun to his head, he looked at the fangs that seemed to stretch from his mouth and reach for him. Carter let the darkness take him and didn't even care about the fact that when found, if they ever found his body, he would be covered in shit as well as piss. He was so fucked.

~~~

Randy was still laughing when they got to their home. The look on the man's face when he'd changed was priceless. He could have done without the smell, of course, but Carter Ravenhall had crapped himself because they had scared him that badly. He looked over at Reid when he cleared his throat. His nod toward Molly made him sober up quickly.

"Honey, we're closer than ever to getting him to pay for what he did." She nodded, but he could feel her pain as if he, too, were hurting. "I'm so sorry, baby. I shouldn't have laughed. I'm sorry."

"He really did kill her." Randy pulled her into his arms and held her as she snuggled into his throat. "He killed her and thought he'd get away with it. Why? What did she do to him that he didn't deserve?"

"He wanted it all and she wasn't going to take it any longer. You gave her that strength." They both looked at Jodie. "When I become a person, I'm not just looking like them but sometimes I take a little of them on. Like your sister. She was so happy to be ending this with him."

"But she's dead because I told her to file for divorce." Jodie shook her head and reached for the strongbox they'd taken from Carter's office. "There is nothing in there that will make me believe that Mary would have left him without my telling her to. She'd be alive had I just kept my —"

"Read that." When she didn't touch it, Jodie picked up the folded paper and opened it for her. This time when she handed it back to her, Molly took it. "It's a contact sheet. Most of those names on there I know. And you should, too, if you're half as good at being a cop as I think you are. But what you might not know is that most of those names are not humans. Most of them, about ninety percent of them, are weres and they're on our list. They're known to be killers."

"So." Molly started to hand it back but at the last second pulled it to her again. "This is dated a year before my sister died. He was looking for someone to kill her back then?"

"I'd say that's a good bet. But look at the papers in the back. You'll see something else." While she thumbed through the last few papers, Randy looked at the ones she'd looked at first. On the first page were the names of nine men who he knew had come through the office where he and Phil worked. He looked at Reid.

"*Yeah, I didn't know if you'd seen them or not. Two, I know for a fact, Phil has tried his best to get put away in one case or another. And there are more on the pages that Molly has now.*" Randy looked over each sheet as it was handed to him from Molly. The names were mounting up and he wanted to contact Phil now, but knew that he'd gone to rest for the day.

"*How did he get this list?*" Reid shrugged and looked at Jodie, who was still talking to Molly. "*You don't think someone we know gave this to him, do you? They would have had to have….*"

It hit him. Just like that he knew who had given this list up. When he was ready to say something about it, Jodie touched his mind. She was still talking to Molly, and he was surprised at that.

"*Don't. Not yet. She has enough to deal with right now, and if you tell her right now, she'll implode. I think she will deal with this in her own way, but if you give him up to her, she might not be as good as we need her to be when the time comes.*" He looked at Molly, who was staring out the window behind them. His heart broke for what she'd have to do now. "*She's a good deal stronger than she looks right now, but with seeing her sister today and dealing with Carter, she has taken too much.*"

Randy knew that her seeing Mary as she'd been hurt had taken a good deal out of her. He'd been having so much fun pretending to be Alice that he'd forgotten what seeing her sister was doing to her. He pulled her closer to him as his brother and Jodie got up to leave. Both of them told him good-bye through their link, but he never said anything to Molly. It was perhaps an hour later when she looked around the room.

"They left?" He nodded. "I guess I'm not a very good hostess right now. I was thinking of Mary and Carter."

"Understandable. You've been dealing with a lot lately." She nodded and stood up to stretch. Randy felt his cock stretch too, and his wolf ran along his skin. She turned to look at him.

"What was that?" He let his wolf go just a little and saw hers come to the surface too. "I can feel her. She's very strong, isn't she? And I think she wants something from me."

"She's as strong as you are. And I suppose that's one way to look at it. She does want something. Me. More when you need her to be, but she's needing her mate too." Molly moved to the doors that led to a private deck at the back of the room. He'd loved that part of this room and was going to ask Molly if he could have this office for his own. He would put in a new desk, but loved the books and the other furniture in here.

"I helped Molly decorate this room. Carter, of course, hated it, but we had so much fun." She walked to the doors and opened them. "When she bought this house, it was planned to be her office. A place for her to come where he wouldn't be able to find her. But after we were finished, we realized it was too masculine for her and she set up the other one across the way."

She stepped out onto the deck, and he watched her. There was something both so sad and very sexy about her right now, and he wanted to see how she worked things out. Leaning against the wrought iron railing, he moved just a little closer to her to hear what she was saying. He wanted to take her where she stood. Mark her with his wolf and fill her with his seed, but he watched her instead, loving her more and more with each passing second.

"The trees back here will be green all year round. She had planned to put a pool here." Her body seemed to sway a little, and he wanted to go to her but stilled when she continued. "I think I'd like to put one in if you wouldn't mind."

"I love the water. And a pool would be nice for the pack we seem to have gotten." She smiled, but it didn't reach her eyes. "We can tell Austin no if you want. He would understand. I'm pretty sure there are any number of others that could help him a good deal more than I would be able to."

"Do you want it?" He found he really did and told her so. "Then that's what I want too. I'm not sure how to be an alpha person, but I was going to talk to CJ about it soon anyway. She seems to have been born to the job. I might never be as good as she is at it, but I can learn. And if they don't like it, then they can go back to Austin or I can shoot them. Either way works for me."

"You have too, been born to the job I mean. When we take a mate, a wolf I mean, they're our equal in every way. Some of them have to have a little training, but alphas, male or female, are born to the job. As for shooting them? I think we should maybe table that one for a last resort kind of way to deal with them. You know? Just leave it out there only if we really need it." She nodded and he moved up behind her. "You should shift. I think your wolf wants out to play."

Her skin was hot to the touch and he knew it was because of her wolf. Their bodies ran a good deal hotter than a human's because of the second body they held. He kissed her neck when she leaned back to him. Her scent made his wolf hum along his skin, and his need for her spiked up again. To make his wolf calm a little, Randy decided to tell her a little about her new self.

"The wolf you have in you will be there when you need her, even when you don't think you do. She'll come to the surface when you're afraid or sometimes when she needs to run. You'll feel that too, the need to run. She'll let you know in subtle ways at first, but then she'll be more aggressive as her needs get stronger." He could feel his wolf as he made his demands too. "My wolf is ready to mark yours."

"I'm not afraid of her." She turned in his arms and looked up at him. "I talked to CJ and the other women the other day. She said she was white, and I heard that one of the others were silver."

"Yes. And she's beautiful as well. I'm wondering if you'll be something extraordinary as well." She kissed his chin and took a step back from him. "Close your eyes and think of her. You should be able to see her there."

"I do. She's...I'm not telling you." He could see the smile on her face and knew that she was going to be a blessing to their pack too. He started to take a step toward her to help her when the air around him tightened. Holding his breath, he watched his mate shift.

"Christ." Randy took another step back from her when she stretched out. She was magnificent. "You're red."

"*I know. I didn't even know there were red wolves.*" He knew that there had been, at one time, a great many of them but now they were all but extinct. He knelt down to her to touch her fur. "*That feels amazing. But I need to run now. I can feel the energy running over me like it's electric. I've never felt this energized before. I feel...hell, I feel fucking fantastic.*"

"Go then. I'll catch up." But she shook her head. "Ah, I see. You want to see me shift? You know that I have to be naked to shift, don't you?"

"*I do. But I think Jodie said something about her giving us a gift. Try it.*" He looked around the decking, just noticing that there were no clothes from Molly's shift. He let go of his wolf and felt the clothing he had on absorb into his body. Christ. Jodie had been very busy lately and he'd have to thank her for it. Blinking several times, he looked at Molly. She was watching him with the most awed expression he'd ever seen. Then she took off. He watched her leap over the steps to the deck in a single bound. It took his breath away.

Randy reached for his brother and Austin as he took off after her. He didn't want to be disturbed when he was with her and wanted them to warn others that they were out. Reid laughed, but Austin told him to be careful. He said that Reid had told him what was going on about who had given them up.

"*I haven't said anything to Molly yet. I want her to know, but it was hard on her today.*" Austin growled low, but it was a friendly kind, not where he was pissed off. "*I know you like her and all, but I'm thinking she'll be okay when she figures it out. She has had a rough time of it lately, and as her mate, I'm going to protect her from this as much as I can. Or until she finds out and tries to murder me.*"

"*I would be careful. I'm pretty sure she'll want a piece of you, and I don't mean in the good way. As for her taking this well, I know she will. The moment I saw her and found out she was your mate, it's when I decided that you'd be the perfect couple to have help me. I'm not saying I'm too old, but the pack is much bigger than I can handle on my own.*" Austin paused. "*I'm thinking you'd rather be with your mate than me trying to talk you into something. Come see me soon. The both of you.*"

Randy agreed and saw his mate. She was leaping over a fallen tree, and he was amazed again at her beauty. Christ, he probably should have told Austin what she was but wanted her to surprise him. And she would. Red wolves, like white and silver ones, were a rarity, and he could not wait for the next pack meeting to introduce her.

Randy moved up behind her only to have her take off again.

"*You're letting me get away.*" He assured her he wasn't, and she laughed. "*I used to do this sort of thing, cat and mouse with some of the guys on the force. They'd never win. And now that I'm a wolf, they'd never find me.*"

"*Some of the men on your force are not human, you know that, right?*" She told him she didn't but had figured it out by now. "*They're mostly wolf and probably didn't play with you when you asked, right?*"

"*That's right. Why not? They could have found me before anyone else, I'm sure.*" He laughed and said they would. "*But I don't understand. Why not put me in my place as a human?*"

"*Because you were special to them and a female of worth. There are few humans that get that kind of treatment and fewer still that are females. And Martin told me that they knew that someday you'd have their back and wanted your confidence to rub off on them. Most of the wolves you worked with are now a member of our pack. We're getting a hell of a force to join us.*"

He saw her again and laid down low to move up behind her. She was upwind from him, and he could smell everything about her...especially her excitement. When he pounced on her, she growled and fought to get away, but his wolf was bigger than hers and a good deal stronger. When she settled, he didn't think she was finished but held her down with his paws.

"*You're hurting me.*" He knew he wasn't and nipped at her shoulder. "*Hey, I thought you weren't supposed to cause me pain? That there was this rule about you having to put me up on a pedestal or something.*"

"*You're not in pain and we both know it. As for being on a pedestal, I'm thinking that if you were there, I'd have a better angle to eat you. You taste delicious when I'm drinking from you. And when my tongue fucks you, I curl it around inside of you to get more of you into my mouth."* He bit her again. *"But you are going to be hurting in a moment. I'm going to fuck you like this."*

He held her down with his mouth as he moved behind her. His cock was aching now and his wolf was getting impatient with her. And him. Every time he would think to take her, she'd move again. Finally, he bit down harder and tasted blood.

"You're going to pay for this." He entered her hard, his wolf growling low as he moved in and out of her. *"I'm going to fuck you again when we shift. But this time it's for my dominance. You've no idea how much fucking you this way pleases me. I'm going to do it again when we're humans. Fuck you like an animal."*

Molly moaned and lifted her ass. Randy felt his wolf approve of his mate and her needs. When he bit down harder as he came, she cried out, and he knew she was coming too. Randy threw back his head and howled as his wolf let him go. He fucked her harder as his cum released into her sheath. She was his.

"Shift for me." She moved back, and he could see the blood on her shoulder. "Come here, Molly, and let me fuck you. I need to fuck you right now. And if you run now, it will not be good for you."

The shift from wolf to human was quick. He moved toward her as he pulled at his clothing. By the time he was standing in front of her, she was naked too and he dropped to his knees. He was going to feast on her, then take her to the ground. But the pain in his back took his breath away, and then he was falling. Her screams made him fight the drug coursing through his body, but he lost the fight almost before it began. Someone had shot him full of a drug and it had to be a lot for it to affect him this way. His final thoughts before it took him was that she was unprotected. His wolf cried out as well.

CHAPTER 9

"I don't know. As I've said to you about three thousand times. I fucking don't know where he is. As soon as I heard the shot, I knew that one of us had to get away or we'd both be dead. Now if you will back the fuck up and let me think, I'll find my mate." Austin took a step back, but he was sure it was because CJ had pulled him back rather than his desire to give Molly what she wanted. Randy was gone, and that's all he could think about. And no one, least of all him, knew where the hell he was.

Austin felt Randy reach for him, but it was cut off almost as soon as he realized who it was. And now he was standing in the area that the two of them had been when he'd been taken. He'd come running when Molly had called for him, and he'd been both terrified and impressed with how calmly she'd told him what had happened.

"We're almost fifty yards from the left corner of the garage as you're facing it. There is a line of trees that run the entire length of the yard, and we entered at the break there. I think we're about ten yards due north from there. They have Randy, but I'm hit too. The drug is strong and I'm fighting to stay awake."

He'd asked her several questions in rapid fire as he shifted and ran for her. He told his family what was going on even as she spoke to him again. She told him that no, she didn't know what kind of drug it was, and she didn't hear anything prior to being shot. But she did tell him to hurry the fuck up. He nearly stumbled when she'd told him that she needed him.

He watched Molly as she fought the effects of the drug. She'd been hit, too, but had pulled the dart free before it had done as much to her as it had Randy. Molly held onto a tree and closed her eyes. He started for her, wanting to make sure she was all right.

"You should be back at the house." She turned and glared at him. "I'm trying my best not to order you to sit the fuck down. You're hurting and we both know it. There isn't anything more you can do here but get in the way. If you don't listen to me, I'm going to have someone take you to the house and tie you to a chair."

"Try it." She turned to look at him and braced her arms over her chest. "Try and order me and see what the fuck I do to you. I'm not one of your pets that will leap through hoops at your command. I'm going to find my mate and when I do, I'm going to go and get him. You get in my way and I swear to Christ I will tear you apart."

Austin felt his anger surge. No one was his pet, and she fucking well knew it. Taking a step toward her, he opened his mouth to command her to shift when Reid was standing in front of him.

"You hurt her and, alpha or not, I will kill you." He knew that the man could, too. He started to take another step toward Molly but stopped when she suddenly sat down. There was something more wrong with her than they'd first thought. She pulled the second dart from her arm and looked at him.

"He got me twice, I guess." Austin moved Reid out of the way and sat before her. She was failing fast, and they all knew it. "I have to tell you everything. I know who it was. Shawn did it."

Austin looked at Jodie when she sat near them and saw that it wasn't a surprise to her in the least. This was getting out of hand. He was sick to death of getting second-hand information from people and getting it a day late to boot. Austin looked at Molly when she growled.

"Can't you be pissy later? Listen to me. He took Randy because he was being threatened by Carter. He's the sniper." Austin saw her face and knew that things were just falling into place for her as she spoke. "He also knew where the money was and had been... Christ. He killed my sister for money."

"He is in a great deal of debt. Gambling mostly. A few years ago he had a huge windfall. We sort of looked into it but not very hard. The information was there on the surface but not all of it." Jodie was talking to Molly, and he had no idea what she was talking about. When she looked at him, he could see her anger. "I should have taken him out when Randy figured out who he was. I was stupid in thinking Molly here couldn't handle any more bad news. She liked Shawn."

"The gun is in the pantry. High on the shelf over the things earmarked to replenish the pantry for your pack." Molly closed her eyes again and swayed hard toward him. He held her up as she continued but knew that he had only seconds to get the information from her. "He and Carter are going to use Randy to get me to come to them. But he didn't count on my being shot twice. I'm assuming that neither knows I'm a wolf."

"No, neither know. I've had Shawn at my home since we had a clue he might be a part of this." Jodie looked at him and smiled. "Shawn thinks you're going to promote him to be your head cook. Little does he know that Nancy is ready to kill him."

"My mom knew?" Molly shook her head, and he laid her back on the ground as the drugs took her. "Now what? Do we go after the bastard and make him tell us where Randy is or wait him out?"

"What do you think Randy would do?" He knew as surely as he was sitting there near his unconscious mate what Randy would do but didn't want to say it to Jodie. She would laugh at him. "Well?"

"He'd say let her rest for a bit. Then when she wakes, let her decide." Jodie laughed. "This is not funny. The longer we wait, the more harm he can cause him. And that kid means a good deal more to me than seeking justice right now. I fucking want his head on a platter."

"And we'll get it. Her way. And Randy will be fine. Trust me." He eyed her closely. She knew something. Christ, when it occurred to him, he nearly shouted the forest down around them.

"You gave them what you have. Both of them." He started to curse but cut himself short. "This is going to save his life, and the only reason I don't impose some sort of fine on you is because I want that kid back. Then I'm going to kick your ass for not telling me when you find shit out. You do know that you're supposed to ask me before you do crazy crap like this."

"Yeah, I know. It's what makes this so much fun." He growled, and Jodie laughed as she continued. "Listen, before we both go off halfcocked and I have to hurt you — again — I wanted to tell you that when Randy and Molly take the pack, Reid and I are going with them. No offense to you, but they're his family and I go where he does. You gonna be all macho about that or you going to be a good man like Reid keeps telling me you are and let us go?"

"Why do you keep making me out to be this asshole when you know that...? I understand. You think this is funny. Well, kiddo, I hope Randy wants to murder you daily like I do." He kissed her on her cheek and heard Reid growl. He had expected them to go to Randy's part of the pack almost in the same moment that he'd thought of Randy being his second alpha. "I'm losing a great deal to him, I think. The ones that have been with me for a long time as well as a few of the younger ones. I thought that I'd let the others choose as well."

"Good thinking." She looked at Molly. "Did you hear what color her wolf is? Reid said Randy wouldn't tell him. They wanted to surprise you."

"Christ. She's going to be polka dotted, isn't she?" Jodie laughed and stood up. When he did as well, he looked around the area again. "There's something here that we're missing. I don't know what it is, but I can feel it."

"Me too. I don't know what, but I have a feeling when she wakes up, she'll tell us right away." She looked at Molly with such pride that he looked too. "Do you know how hard she had to work at staying awake with two darts in her? The strength it took for her to wait on us to get here alone cost her. I'm proud to have her as my sister."

It didn't take her long to wake. Molly was laying there as quiet as a leaf. Then suddenly she was sitting up. Austin watched her and knew the moment she'd seen whatever it was that he and Jodie and the rest of the pack hadn't. When she stood up, three of his brothers helped her. Gordon started laughing.

"Randy is going to be pissed when he gets back." Molly asked him why. "Because, my dear alpha person, you're going to have the scent of another male on you. Several of them as a matter of fact. Do you know what he's going to have to do to get the scent off you? He's going to have to mark you all over again. Both him and his wolf."

It took her a few seconds to get it but when she did, her face brightened up a great deal. Austin might have laughed at her, but she was beating on Gordon and he wasn't sure he wanted her to hit him that hard. Instead, he put his fingers in his mouth and let out a loud whistle. Everyone stood still.

"What do you see?" Molly walked over to where she'd told them all she and Randy had been standing. She leaned over and picked up a long chain. Holding it up, he nearly laughed out loud when he saw what was on the end. "It's a safety deposit key. And if I don't miss my guess, I'm betting it's to the bank we own."

"Yeah. I think whoever owns this key is going to have a lot of explaining to do." Molly dropped it in the baggie that Jodie held out. "Could you send three pack members to the bank and see...why are you shaking your head at me?"

"Because any man or woman here is going to pledge to you as soon as it's official. You send your pack. Mine is here to find Randy." Molly looked around, panic stricken. "You can do this. Just treat them the way you'd want to be treated."

Austin watched her as she moved to a group of men and nearly laughed when they all bowed before her. They were hers and Randy's, and that was it. He listened to her ask them to see to the key and tell two of them go and watch Shawn. The rest she sent to the house to make sure that Carter didn't move in while she was busy. She then sent some to gather more pack and watch all the houses. She said she wasn't taking any chances with her family.

"Also, I'm going to need ten men or women to be a mainstay in our household. You'll need to be able to help with the everyday life of the house as well as be ready at a moment's notice to draw arms. I have a feeling that with the money we have now people are going to get it into their heads that we're fair game. You can decide. And when Randy gets home, we'll go over it with everyone." Austin watched them to see of anyone would tell her no. But all of them, even the three he had expected to balk at the idea of doing housework, nodded to her as they took off to do her bidding. Austin knew then that he'd made the right choice. He just hoped that they did as well.

They scattered, and she was left standing there looking into the woods. He wanted to ask her about the key and why it had stayed hidden until she woke, but wasn't sure he wanted her to answer that. There were things that Jodie and Reid did that scared the shit out of him, and he had a feeling that Molly was going to be no different. When she turned around, he could see the determination on her face as well as some of the drug still there. He didn't move when she wiped at tears on her cheeks. Some things were better left alone.

He looked at her when she walked toward him. She'd changed in the few minutes she'd been asleep. The woman before him was not just stronger than she'd been before all this, but she was a good deal more confident in her abilities. When she smiled at him, he was proud of her. She was going to be one hell of a leader.

"Let's go and get my mate. I'm looking forward to him marking me up again and this time, without the guns going off around us making me feel like I'm drunk as shit." He wrapped his arm around her shoulders and pulled her to him. She laughed as she continued. "You're doing that on purpose, aren't you?"

"I am. And I'm having the time of my life thinking of other ways to piss Randy off when he gets home. This is going to be more fun than I ever imagined." He laughed again. "And don't be surprised if a few of the females make it so you want to mark him right back."

Her low growl had him laughing out loud. Yes, Austin thought this was going to be a great deal of fun. Then he remembered while he'd been marking her, her scent was all over him. Smiling, he thought of ways his own mate might want to mark him. Austin was nearly skipping when they went back to the house.

~~~

Randy felt the chains around his ankles and kept his eyes closed. He reached out into the room and could feel that while he was alone in the little room, there were several others just beyond where he was. Opening one eye, he looked around without raising his head and could see that the floor was simply a concrete slab and that what he could see of the walls told him that they were made of the same material. Lifting his head a little more, he could see light from the doorway but nothing else. Wherever he was, it was deep within a place that he couldn't get out of easily. He looked down at his body and did a quick inventory of what they'd done to him.

Drugs. That was all he could find at the moment, but he'd not moved. He didn't think he'd been hurt much. A bump on his head, more than likely caused from being tossed into something like a car or van. His head was fuzzy, but again, nothing more than the drugs that were slowly dissipating had caused. Even his clothes looked okay, other than a few missing buttons. Then he remembered that he'd been naked when he'd been shot and smiled. He wondered who had dressed him and if they had been embarrassed by it. He knew he would have been if the shoe was on the other foot.

The chains were biting into his flesh, both around his ankles and his wrist. Whoever had him knew that silver was poisonous to his kind, and he could only think of one person who would do this to him. Shawn had a great deal to pay for when he found him again. And this time, Randy was not going through the proper channels to make sure he did.

Randy knew that Molly had run from them when he'd been shot. He was proud of her for thinking like that. If they both had been caught, he was sure they'd both be dead. There was no way he was going to die here. Randy smiled when he felt her touch his mind.

"Do you know where you are?" He could hear her humor. He smiled again when he thought of her. He sent her mental images of them together and what he wanted to do to her when they were together again. She laughed harder. *"Behave or I'll let you rot there. Now get busy helping me find you before I have to murder Austin. You never know a person until you have to spend too much time with them. He's like an old woman when it comes to his pack."*

"He's a good guy when he wants to be. Is he trying to get you to do things his way? I'm pretty sure that he is going to lose

on that one. You can be pretty stubborn when you wish to be." He leaned his head back on the wall and thought of where he was and what he could do to aid her in finding him. "*I don't know. Concrete is all I can see right now, and there are no windows to the outside. I can, however, smell the panther and the wolf outside the door, but I don't know either of them.*"

Randy reached out to their mind and found nothing more than a game they were discussing. There were bits and pieces of information about Shawn, which he passed on to Molly, but little else. Most of it had to do with how much of a pain in the ass he was.

"*They think he's a dick. I'm sure they're right. The panther is afraid he's going to try to kill the leader of their leap. Austin told me what a group of panthers was called when I met my first panther shifter.*" He put his foot out when he saw something on the floor in front of him. "*I want to kick Shawn's ass when we find him again. He will pay for this shit. I was having a good time, and he fucked it all up for us.*"

"*You'll have to stand in line to kick him around. After I'm finished with him, I think Nancy wants to have a go at him. And she said the wooden spoon will be the least of his problems. She's sort of scary, isn't she?*" He smiled as he was able to get the shiny piece of metal toward him. It took him three tries, but he finally had it where he could make it out. A small paperclip. He'd used less as a teenager to get into things he shouldn't have. Moving it more, he finally got it up onto his leg and had to nearly bend himself in half to get it into his hand.

"*She can be. Just before I left for college she sat me down with that spoon between us. She told me that I was going to know the brunt of it if I failed a single class. I believed her. She is this sweet most wonderful person one second, but you know that in a heartbeat she'll cut you to ribbons.*" He put the paperclip in his mouth and bent it. It had been years, almost a decade, since he'd had to rob anyone for a place to stay or food. He hoped that he'd remember enough to get out of this for Molly.

"I think I have you located, or at least close to where you might be. I can almost see you there. Do you smell anything besides the others? Like sewage?" He raised his head up and opened his mouth to let more of the air come into his body. He told her no. *"Okay, try this. Do you hear anything?"*

He listened, not just with his ears but with his body. It was a trick he'd learned in college. There were times when he'd get turned around on campus and would have to think his way back to his dorm. When he heard the sound of a door slamming, he wondered if someone had joined the party outside but realized it wasn't. There were several men talking in low tones, and all it centered on loads…like a trucker would carry on a truck, not like they were carrying them personally. He could hear engines running too. Diesel, if he didn't miss his bet.

"I think I'm near a truck stop. Or something like it. There's one out on seventy-nine. I think it's called Mother Truckers." He laughed when she did. *"Might not be it, but that's all I can think of. One of the men is talking about the weather he's going to run into. Another is talking about scrambled eggs and steak. Christ, I just realized how hungry I am."*

He moved the paperclip to the lock above his head and felt the sweat roll down his face. He was hot, unseasonably so. He started to tell Molly that when he thought of something else. Randy smiled when he thought of the things that mean something when you're desperate.

"I found a paperclip. I think I'm in some sort of storeroom. Or what might have been one at one time." He looked around again, this time searching the floor and corners instead of looking for a window. *"There is an ink pen that's covered in*

dust, and I can see several more paperclips scattered around the room. Yeah, I'm thinking that at one time, the area I'm in was a storage room for office supplies. And the size of this room makes me think it was a big building. This room is about the size of our pantry but taller."

He could see the scrape marks on the floor, like a shelving unit had been moved instead of picked up. The harder he looked the more he saw that made him think he was correct. In addition to the pen and clips he also saw a file that was plastered to the wall, as well as an index card. He wondered what else he might find if he were to find a broom and start using it.

"*There's a building near a truck stop about fifteen miles from where you were picked up. It's a large building and has been for sale for a long time. Austin said that he wanted to buy it, but the owner didn't seem to be inclined to sell. We're looking it up now to see who owns it.*" He heard her laughter. "*Have you gotten that lock opened yet?*"

He turned the clip twice more before he heard the click. He knew that the others outside the room were too busy arguing about a game that was on to hear him, but he waited all the same. He grinned when he wondered how she knew what he was doing.

"*That nice little extra your sister-in-law gave us. I thought if I distracted you enough you'd not think about how hard it was going. I need you to be free to help me find you.*" She laughed again. "*You can't expect me to do all the work, can you?*"

Randy stood but was careful where he walked. He wasn't going to give himself away until he had to. He glanced out the little window over the door and couldn't see shit. The foggy glass was so dirty that he thought it a miracle that he could get any light in the room he was in at all. The wire through the glass also didn't help but distorted the view to the other side a great deal.

"There are four blurs on the other side of the room where I am. I can see that the television is on, but I don't hear any sound. I'm assuming that's so they can hear me if I try to escape. I can't make out what they are, but I think in addition to the panther and wolf, there is at least one human. The four of them are sitting around a table and I can smell pizza." Randy tried not to think about how long it had been since he'd eaten. *"When you get here, I don't suppose you can bring me a sandwich, could you? I'm starving."*

"Nancy is working on a party of some sorts. I'm not sure what it's about, but it looks like there is enough food here for about a thousand people. When I ask about it, all I get is a pat on the head and a smile." Molly was quiet for a little while and he used the time to clean a little of the window at the bottom. He was right, there were four people in the room beyond.

"What's wrong?" He asked the question and meant for her to answer him, but when she didn't, he paused. There was something going on that had her terribly upset. *"Molly?"*

"She's really gone. Mary. She's gone and...what will I do now?" He was wondering what had happened when she continued. *"We'll have her killer, and her ex-husband will go to jail. But then what? She's still gone. And I still don't understand the reasons behind her having to die. He didn't even love her."*

Randy wasn't sure what to say to her, so he told her how he felt. *"I love you so much. I know this is stupid timing, but I do. And I want to be with you, hold you and keep you safe. I know, I know, you can protect me, but I still want to keep you in my heart forever. I think that once this shit is over we should go away for a while. I'm sure we can go anywhere we want. Where would you like to go?"*

"*Somewhere we need passports for. What if...how about we visit the world? You know, Ireland, Scotland? Then we can go to Paris and London. Have you ever been there? And just so you know, I love you too.*"

Randy knew that he had to get out of there. He had to get to her and show her how much he really did love her and needed her. Kneeling down in front of the door with his paperclip, he started trying to pick the lock. "*Just will it open, Reid said. He said that they've given us a little more than we had and that you should be able to will it open. When this is over, maybe we should hunt them down and beat the shit out of them. Some of this stuff we're supposed to be able to do is some fucked up shit. Hey! I think we found you. We're on our way.*"

Will it open? And what does he mean they've "given us a little more?" "*More? More what, did anyone tell you? You're right, we're so going to have a talk with them when I get there.*" He put his hand on the lock and heard it click. Knowing that the others on the other side of the door more than likely heard it too, he stood up and slammed the door open so that it hit the wall hard. The room looked like a dorm room, with crushed empty beer cans and several empty pizza boxes. Slobs was all he could think of.

As they turned to him, they had the most shocked looks on their faces that he'd ever seen. Randy thought this might be really funny if they hadn't been so armed. When he stepped into the room with them, he smiled. This might be fun. Bracing his arms over his chest, he grinned bigger. These guys were going to pay. But first....

"Hello there. Do you think one of you could direct me to the way out of here? My mate is on her way and I'd really like to finish what you fuckwads interrupted."

The guy in the middle looked confused. There were two others sitting at the table with him and one standing at the cooler with a beer in his hands. It was still poised halfway to his mouth. Randy took a step toward them when they suddenly seemed to come alive.

He hit the guy with the beer in the face just as he dropped the can on the floor. A surge of power came over him, and it was over almost too soon for him. Looking around at the four dead men, he wondered just what it was that his family had given them. Not that he was complaining right now, but damn, he'd never felt like this before.

Turning when the door opened behind him, he lifted his fists. Molly was engulfing him into her arms almost as soon as he realized it was her. Holding her as tightly as he could, he rained kisses all over her and told her in between them how much he loved her. His life was suddenly very complete.

CHAPTER 10

"I want my lawyer." The judge kept looking over the file, ignoring him. Carter wasn't used to people simply not doing what he told them. But it was happening more and more lately, and he wasn't happy about it. Standing up, he glared at the man. "I demand that you put that file down and listen to what I am requesting of you."

The judge, a man by the name of Jackson Sable, put down the file. Carter started to smile at him. He was glad now that he'd perfected the tone he'd used on him by having servants running around doing his bidding. But it was short lived when Jackson picked up his gavel and pointed it at him.

"Sit your butt down right now and keep your trap shut. If you so much as whisper another single word, I will find you in contempt and have you hauled over to county lock-up. In the event it might have escaped your notice, you're not in charge here. I am, and I take my job very seriously." Carter started to protest and had opened his mouth to say something, but the look in the judge's eye gave him second thoughts. He sat down and shut up, for now. Something just had to go his way. He was sick of being on the losing end of everything.

Like the fact that he'd been in jail for the past week. And not one of those kinds where you wear your own clothes and have the run of the yards. He'd seen that on television once and wanted that for him. It was bad enough that he was in lock-up, but to be put with such low-lifes was more than he could stand. He was going to talk to his congressman when he was let out of there. There was no reason the state couldn't afford to put men like him, former football players and men who'd been married to big-time celebrities, in something more…accommodating. Like a nice hotel with room service. He missed his nightly glass of chardonnay too. When the door opened behind him, he turned.

"Mother fuck." He looked at the judge to see if he had heard him. He had, and if the glare was any indication, he was going to follow through on his threat. Carter now knew enough about county lock-up to know that he'd never survive another hour there, much less another night. He'd made himself a few enemies before leaving in the car. A couple of them told him he'd be lucky if he made it through the day. Carter knew he wasn't as young and fit as he'd once been and was terrified of going back. It was why he had to win today. But the people who just came in were going to put him there sure as shit.

"Your honor." Jackson nodded at Molly as she sat down. An immaculately dressed man sat at the table opposite where Carter had been seated. He set an expensive briefcase down on the table as the judge greeted him as well. Who the fuck was Randal Atkins? The two other people who sat with him looked like they were one of those couples you'd see on the top of a wedding cake, all soft and in love. It was sickening. To him the word love was something you said to a woman to get her to suck your cock, not make a lifetime of hell over.

The door opened again, and this time a man came rushing in, still stuffing papers into his bag. It wasn't even a brief case but a worn backpack that had seen better days. The man nearly slipped on his shoelace and had to stop twice on his way to the front of the courtroom to pick up his glasses and an ink pen. He made the others look even better, if that was possible. Whoever he was there for, Carter almost felt sorry for them.

"I'm sorry I'm late, your honor. I just got word that I was supposed to be here. I'm the public defender you asked for." The judge told him not to worry, things were already delayed. "My client, sir, do you think I can have a moment to go over a few things with him? I promise you, I won't take more than a few minutes."

At the judge's nod, Carter found himself being jerked from his chair and pulled along between two officers to a room just off the dais. As he was shoved into a chair, the public defender came in as well. He was just pulling out a stack of messy papers when it occurred to Carter what was going on.

"You're not defending me." The kid, because he would swear the man was only in his early teens, looked at him with a frown. "You get your ass out of here right now and find my lawyer. I want him, not some jack wipe that is still not shaving. This is ridiculous. I was married to one of the most famous actresses in the world. You're not defending me, and I certainly do not need a freebie lawyer. You get out of here."

"I'm really sorry you feel that way, Mr. Ravenhall. And I thought your ex-wife was an amazing actress, despite being saddled with you. But as it is, you have me."

The voice was in direct contrast to the one he'd used in the courtroom. This time he sounded hard and without any compromise. Carter lifted his brow at him. He didn't have to take this shit from a snot-nosed kid like this one.

"You tone that shit down right now or find yourself out of a job. I don't care what you think you're going to do here, but I have a lawyer. A fucking amazing lawyer, and I will use him. I do not now, nor will I ever leave my fate in the hands of someone who gets paid minimum scale. I know my funds are a little on the lean side right now, but I will not tolerate this bullshit from a public defender. His name is Donald James, and he's with—"

"I'm well aware of who your lawyer was when you had a wife whom you abused. But you are no longer being represented by his firm. As of the day before yesterday, his firm has disassociated themselves with you and this case. That is why I'm here. Furthermore, they have told the courts that you still owe them for services that have been billed for over six months." Carter opened his mouth to deny that but was cut off again. "My name is Peterson, David Peterson, and I work for the courts system. As your lawyer, I suggest you plead guilty of all the charges brought against you. I've seen what they have and there is enough against you as of this moment to have you put on death row without any chance of parole. And if they have their way, which I'm sure it's going to go that way, you'll be put to death sooner rather than later. You're fucking with the wrong attorney out there if you think you can win. But if you plead out, there is a chance that I can—"

"Now you listen here. I'm not going to admit to anything I didn't do. I didn't kill my wife. She wasn't anywhere near me when it happened. I was in bed with the housemaid, fucking her stupid. And I was tested with one of those test things and there was no gun residue on my hands." Carter started to stand and was shoved back into the seat. "I will not put up with this kind of treatment. I don't know where you get off thinking you can treat me as a commoner, but I don't have to put up with this. Get me my lawyer right fucking now."

Carter waited for the man to say something, but he sat there for so long that Carter felt himself squirm. It wasn't the fact that he wasn't speaking to him, but he was looking at him as if he were a slug. No one looked at him like that again. Then he spoke.

"The charges brought against you are as follows…and I'd pay attention if I were you. The judge will expect you to have a plea for each one. Murder in the first degree for one Sandra Middleton, age seventeen; murder in the first degree of Mary Barker Ravenhall, age twenty-nine; attempted murder of—"

"Who?" The man looked at his papers when Carter asked him again. "That Middleton person? Who the hell is that? I didn't kill her. You got it all wrong. See, this goes to prove how wrong you are for this job. You don't even have the right people I'm supposed to be on trial for. And the way you're dressed, it screams unfit for the position. I will not ask you again to get me my lawyer."

Papers shuffled, and when David found whatever it was he'd been looking for, he smiled at him. "Her name was Sandra Middleton, and you killed her when you were in a drunken rage during an altercation at the time with Mary Barker and her sister, Molly. You claimed that the car was defective and that it slipped from park and that was how it came to run over her. But after further investigation it was found to have been a lie. You are now being held responsible for her death as well as that of Ms.

Ravenhall." David cleared his throat and looked him over again. "As for how I'm dressed? Have you had an opportunity to look in a mirror lately, Mr. Ravenhall? You look as if you were laying with tramps."

Which was true. He had been. And now he could smell it on his body like one of his favorite scents. Not to mention he'd not had his hair groomed this week. However, a man was supposed to look...Carter took a deep breath and let it out slowly. He was not going to let this man rattle him again. He thought about who he was supposed to have murdered instead of acting out and murdering this man as well.

"That kid? You're bringing that into this now?" David nodded, and Carter laughed. "You do know that was over ten years ago, right? That girl is probably dust by now, and you think you can press those charges against me after all this time? Get real. Her own parents have probably forgotten about her by now. She was nothing, and no one cared about her death then and certainly don't now."

"Mr. Ravenhall, there is no statute of limitations on aggravated murder. Actually, on any sort of murder. And when you factor in that your blood-alcohol rate was point two-one, and you were a minor, you're looking at hard time on that alone." Carter started to lunge for the man but was shoved back again. This was ridiculous. They couldn't do this to him. But David continued before he could speak. "Her parents have expressed a desire to have your head hung from a pike in their yard. They plan to burn your picture in effigy daily while the trial is going on. As a matter of fact, they seem to think you should be roasted on a spit in their yard. Alive."

David sat down after straightening his ill-fitting suit. He took several deep, slow breaths that he let out just as slowly, seemingly counting to ten as he did this. Carter nearly slapped him to get him back on track, but David looked at him in a way that Carter knew if he touched the man, he'd be picking his ass up off the floor in a heartbeat. David picked up his paperwork and began reading again.

"As I was saying, attempted murder of one Molly Barker, detective first class, the kidnapping and attempted murder of one Randal Atkins, attorney." Carter started to stand again, stating that he didn't know who this man was either, when David explained. "He is the man you had kidnapped to bring Molly to heel, as we were told. You really did screw the pooch on this one, didn't you? One of the most powerful families in the world, not to mention a man worth billions, and you tried to kidnap him. You must be the stupidest man alive."

Carter lunged again, and this time he got his hands around David's throat. As he was being dragged away from him, David laughed. This was not what he had expected. Nor did he expect the man to tell the cops to let him go. He then asked all but one of them to leave him. Carter thought that they were going to use him as a punching bag or something. But David sat down again.

"I'm not human."

Carter started to ask him what the fuck he was talking about when suddenly there was a large panther in the room with him. When he shifted back, Carter moved back, glad that the cop was still in the room with them.

"You think you can scare me with your bully tactics? I got news for you, dumb shit. I'm scarier than you'll ever be on your best days. Now sit your fat ass down and shut the fuck up. If you don't, I'm going to have Charlie here, who is a lion by the way, tear you a new ass while he drinks your fucking blood from your still beating heart. And when he's finished with you, he and I will dispose of your body and tell them you got away. No one will care because they'll know that you've been taken care of. Now this is what we're going to do. We're going to go out into the courtroom, you'll hear the charges brought up against you again, and this time you'll either nod your head at the judge or shake that incredibly empty space between your shoulders. Either way, you're going to go to prison for a very long time, if not the chair for all this. And I, for one, will be seated in the first row so I can smell you when you shit yourself."

Carter nodded when he was asked something, but all the time he was trying to figure out how to get out of this. He had money at the mansion and as soon as they let him go and get it he was going to use it to pay off whoever he had to. This was just stupid. He'd been married to one of the most beautiful women in the world according to one tabloid, and now he was being represented by a...well, he wasn't really sure what he was, but Carter wasn't going to jail. Jail was for criminals, and he most certainly was not. He was an opportunist.

Once it was declared that he was set to go, he was picked up and dragged back into the courtroom. He stumbled twice when he saw who was seated in the front row with Molly. Then something else occurred to him. His Mary was there. Mary had come to the courtroom to see him, and he waved at her with a grin. If she wasn't dead, there was no way for them to charge him with her murder. As soon as he was seated, he stood up and looked at the judge.

"Your honor. My wife is not dead. As you can see, the fool that I hired to kill her fucked up and she's sitting right there." They all looked to where he was pointing, then back at him. "And I bet if you look really hard you'll see that the other one…somebody Middletown…is alive too."

No one said a word, and he put out his cuffed hands. They'd have to let him go now. There wasn't a dead body for him to have killed, so they were going to have to let him go. And if Mary was alive, then the house was his again. He looked over at Molly. He was certainly going to make her wish she was dead after all she'd put him through. But for now, he'd play nicely. He did look at Molly, who looked confused.

"I'll expect you to be moved out by the end of the day. I don't know what sort of damage you did to my house, but you'll be hearing from my attorney, a real one this time, to pay for any and all damages." He smiled when she looked to her left as if she didn't see her sister sitting there. "You won't think this is so funny when I take everything you ever hope to have. Your sister and I are going to have a grand old time getting reacquainted. I might even knock her up. With my dick this time, not my fist."

"What are you talking about?" Carter looked at the judge, who was standing over the dais looking down on him as he spoke. It might have been funny, his look of utter disbelief, if Carter wasn't sure somehow they were all in on this. "Did you just admit to hiring someone to murder your wife and shoot your sister-in-law?"

Carter had to think. Had he done that? Probably. But it was a moot point now as she wasn't dead. Neither them were. So he nodded. Jackson sat down again and looked around the room as if he couldn't believe it either. Carter stretched out his hands again. The sooner they took these cuffs off, the sooner he could get back to his old life.

"Didn't you go to the funeral of your late wife? I was there, I'm pretty sure, like the rest of us, we saw her, too." Carter nodded, smiling. He had no idea how she'd pulled it off, but the judge was right, he'd been acting the grieving widower at her funeral. "And during all this time, you've been under the assumption that she's been alive? You've seen her before today?"

"On no, your honor. I thought she was dead until she started showing up recently. You see, she's a really good actress, all the important people said so. So she's been laying low until she showed up in my bathroom while I was shaving the other morning. She asked me if I was...I don't remember what she said, but she told me she was...she loved me." Several people snickered behind him, and he turned on them. "You should have seen her. I was shocked too. But she was in my limo as well as my office, too. She sat there looking like she always does, beautiful and made up to look like a star. I've been seeing her a lot over the past week. I'm pretty sure once this mess is over, she and I will go back to the way things were."

"In your dreams." The voice whispered over his cheek, and he felt the hot breath. There was no one there, but he heard Mary speak to him. When he started to say something to the judge about her being there now, he looked over at Molly again and saw Mary still sitting there. The woman in the front, the one with the other man, turned and was talking to Molly. Both of them were shaking their head and looking at him. Then Mary walked through them. Just stood up and came toward him and blew him a kiss before she disappeared again, looking like someone had shot her head all up. Carter sat down.

"I don't feel so well." Jackson asked him what was wrong. "I don't know. I can see her sitting over there, and she looks like somebody hurt her. It wasn't me this time. At least I don't think so. Maybe it was Shawn who shot her again. He told me he was the best. It was why I kept him around. He was who I hired when things didn't go my way. But this is making me sick and my heart is hurting again. I think maybe I'm having a heart attack. Christ, I hurt. Do you think I can have a nitro pill? I have them in my coat pocket."

Two men stepped forward as his head started to spin. Carter could feel his heart pounding like someone had put a battery on it and turned it up to full force. Plus, he was dizzy and that, too, was making him sick to his stomach. He put his hand over his mouth, or at least tried to, but nothing was working right. When his mouth was pried open, he felt the little pill being shoved under his tongue. Carter had a feeling it was too late, and he was afraid. He dropped his head on the table as his body began to shut down. When the pain in his head exploded, Carter opened his eyes, and his last vision was his wife laughing at him.

~~~

He was dead. Carter Ravenhall was dead and now it was about over. Except that Molly knew things would never be the same again. She stared out the window as people talked behind her. When she felt someone come up beside her, she turned and looked at Nancy Force.

"You should eat something." Molly didn't say anything. She'd been telling people she wasn't hungry for the past two days. She just wanted them to leave her alone. "There are things that need to be said between the two of us. Would you mind going to the kitchen with me?"

"There's some sort of meeting going on in there. The staff is trying to figure out who I should hire as the next cook. Apparently none of them cared all that much for Shawn in the first place. Not even his wife. Did you know that she was forced to marry him because he wanted to fuck her? Never mind. I just thought of that and for some reason my filter is all fucked up." Molly saw a deer run across the yard and watched its progress as she continued. "I don't really have anything to add to what is going on, Mrs. Force. I'm sort of just waiting for them to tell me what I do. I've been dealing as best I can, but I'm just...I'm really tired right now."

"You're being lazy." She supposed she was but didn't rise to the bait of her angry words. "Are you just going to waste away to nothing while your mate's heart breaks? Is this how you love someone? Look at that poor boy. He doesn't know what to do to help you, and you're not giving him what he needs. Love is a give-and-take sort of thing. Where is your giving?"

"I really think you should back the fuck off. I'm dealing with a lot of shit right now and I don't want to say something to you I might regret." The pain in her head had her whipping around so quickly that she had to steady herself. Nancy was holding the spoon out like she was going to bonk her again when Molly took a step back. "What the fuck is wrong with you? Do you know how much I've lost in the past month?"

"I do. And what will sulking do to improve your lot in life? Nothing. You're hurting the people around you and you don't even seem to care." The spoon lashed out and hit her between the eyes this time, and Molly had to sit down. "Is there anything up there in that head of yours, or are you simply using it to hold up your hair?"

Molly felt the tears pool in her eyes as she sat there. "My family is all gone. What the hell am I supposed to do now? Have a party? Or would you like for me to go dancing tonight because everything worked out? It's gone. All of it is gone."

Nancy sat down next to her but didn't put the spoon away. Her voice was softer now and full of pain. So much so that Molly could feel it coursing through her own body and heart. "And again, how is sulking going to make that any different? You don't think all of us have lost someone? My mate left me when I had five children to raise. The youngest three were still in diapers when he died. And Austin and Dallas lost their father too. Holly lost her daddy, the man she thought would be there forever for her. How do you think that affected their lives? Look at CJ, her father...well, we won't use him as an example. He was a turd-head and made everyone miserable. But each of us have lost our family and we're for the most part better for it. What did Mary want from you?"

"Want from me? She's dead, how could she want anything?" The spoon hit her again and she glared. "I'm going to use that on you if you do that to me again. That fucking hurts and I'm sure you know it. If not, I can show you."

But she thought about what she'd asked her. What did Mary want from her? She'd made sure that she had everything she had. It was more than she wanted or even knew what to do with. She and Randy had yet to decide what to do with the house. But for now, they were having the house appraised as well as the contents. Not because she thought they'd sell it. The pool people were supposed to come by tomorrow and give them an estimate on how much it would cost to put one in. And they'd interviewed several pack members who said they'd keep their lawns for them. She and Randy had decided to help some of the younger pack members get businesses started, like pool services as well as lawn care ones.

"She was such a wonderful person." Nancy nodded and leaned back. "And when she was on the big screen, I was never more proud of anyone than I was her. She could make you believe whatever she was portraying up there and you'd walk out knowing that she believed it too. I'd help her with lines at night. She'd call me and have me read some stupid part she had to learn. We'd do more laughing than anything. I'm going to miss her."

"This house, what does it mean for you?" Her first thought was memories, but she knew that wasn't what Nancy meant. Molly looked out the window again and imagined the pool there with lots of kids and adults hanging around it. There were hot dogs for the kids and thick steaks for the adults. The whole house could be decorated for Christmas, not just their special room. She'd see about having Thanksgiving here as well as parties for Memorial Day and the Fourth. The house could heal her, she thought, not just flood her with memories.

"When she first took me through it, all I could think about was this is what Carter wanted, not her. She gushed over some of the rooms but not as much as she did his office. We worked for months on getting the desk that's in her office. Carter hated it on sight. I guess we both knew he would too. But we decorated it because we wanted to, not because a decorator told us what to do with it." She looked around the room they were in now as she continued. "We spent so much time in this room together when I'd come to visit. She and I would have our own

Christmas and Thanksgiving in here. It was silly because there was the huge dining room, but we would do it all the same. Our presents weren't expensive. One year I got her a framed picture of the two of us as children. I think this house would be a balm to a lot of people in the pack, a place where there can be merriment." Molly flushed. "You must think I'm a sap."

"I don't think that at all. I think it's wonderful and something your sister would have loved." Nancy reached for the picture and looked at it before handing it to her. "You two look a great deal alike. I never realized that before. I'm surprised they didn't use you as a double for her sometimes. Did you ever think Mary would be so famous?"

"Oh yes," Molly said without hesitation. "She was forever playacting and standing in front of a mirror to practice her face. That's what she called it, face practice. And it wasn't like she was vain. She wasn't, but she was going to be someone someday, and she wanted to be an actress. And I never believed for one minute that she'd be anything but that. She made me want it for her."

"She was very good at her craft. What will you do with yours?" Molly put the picture back, thinking about her craft. She had no idea what Nancy was talking about but assumed she meant being a cop.

"I'm supposed to interview for a position on the force here in town. I go in on Monday morning." Nancy cocked a brow at her, something she'd seen all her sons do. "If that's not what you mean, then I don't understand. I don't have a craft."

Her laughter had the room turning toward them and Molly was slightly embarrassed. "Oh my dear, you have a very fine craft. And once you figure it out, I hope I'm there to see you use it again and again."

Molly had no idea what she was talking about and looked around the room. They were all there. Most of them had been there when she and Randy had gotten up...Nancy had been making breakfast for them. The others, with their children and nannys, had shown up just as another run was made on the pantry Nancy was helping her set up. And they'd brought more food. Now they sat around laughing and joking with each other as if there was a trial tomorrow for what they had considered one of their own.

"They love each other, don't they?" She didn't wait for Nancy to answer her but continued. "Austin isn't just their leader but truly their brother. And not just to the men here but to the women as well. Dallas is so amazing that no one looks at his limp. They only see the strength of the man standing with them. Connor and Gordon try so hard to be like them both, going so far as to mimic his every movement and his advice. And Holly...she has her own strength, that seems to be a pride and a burden to all of them. You know what I mean?"

"Yes, she does. And Phil is the perfect foil for her antics too. As for Austin, they've always looked up to him. Not just because he's the oldest but because he's always been there for them." Molly nodded at Nancy as she pointed to Myles. "He was so lost when they brought him here. His body alone was destroyed by the man who killed him."

"Killed him?" Nancy nodded. "You mean he's not always been a vampire? I thought...I have no idea why I thought he'd been born one, like Phil was. He seems so...I guess so natural at being what he is. Like he was supposed to be that since birth."

"Oh no. He was helping to save one of my daughters when he was torn apart. It was save him or let him die. But he'd come to mean so much to them, especially Phil and Holly, that they couldn't let him be gone from them forever. Myles had a hard time of it, of course, but they have brought him around. And he's done a fine job of it as well. I'm very proud of him and the others."

"Phil terrifies me." As if he knew she was talking about him, he turned and winked at her. "I think he knows when I'm doing something I shouldn't, and...I've altered my thoughts about things when I think he might come for me because of it. I have no idea why I think that of him. He seems like such a nice guy, but there is something very...murderous, I guess, about him that makes me think he'd stop at nothing if he thought an injustice had been done."

"He'd never harm you. None of them would." Molly turned to look at her, and Nancy put her spoon into her hand, wrapping her fingers around it and her hand. "Don't you know by now that you're very important to them? That they think of you as much of a sister as they do Holly? You might not have been born to this family, but you are family to all of us."

Molly looked down at the spoon, then back up at Nancy. "No. I don't understand you guys. None of you. Randy even, at times, makes me think I'm in a dream and will be awakened from it soon and I'll find this is all just that, a dream."

Holly came and sat beside her. She smiled as she wrapped her arm around her shoulder. "I can hear you. All of us can. We want you to know that this is no dream.

And more so, that any and all of us would die for you. You should also know that when this is over, the trial, your house set to rights, Lou, Alexis, CJ, Stacey and Chris, and I are taking you out on the town. We're going to buy you things you'll be too embarrassed to try on for us, but Randy will love."

She looked at Jodie, who hadn't been included. Molly loved this woman as much as she had her own sister. Nancy laughed, and Molly turned to her. Her grin seemed to take up her entire face.

"Who do you think is going to be watching over us when we go? Jodie has already claimed shotgun." Molly looked at Jodie again. She had a feeling that her version of shotgun wasn't what she'd grown up thinking it was. The person in the front seat with the driver was probably not what Jodie had in mind.

"Should I be more afraid now?" Holly laughed, and the men, especially her mate, turned to look at her. Holly nodded and hugged her again. "Yeah, that's what I was afraid of."

CHAPTER 11

There were more people in this building than Randy thought there had ever been just simply walking in and out of it in a years' time. He was glad now that someone had suggested using the empty building on Fourth Street rather than the smaller one they usually used for pack meetings. Randy looked around again just to be sure that someone was manning the exits. If there was a problem, he wanted to make sure that everyone was going to get out. He saw Molly enter just as the bailiff was closing the doors.

"She'll be fine." Randy turned to look at Phil. The man had been sitting next to him so quietly that he'd forgotten about him until he spoke. "Molly will do us all proud. You should know that. This will go like clockwork and when it's done, our world will be that much safer."

"I do. But I still worry for her." He did too. And until this was settled, and maybe after, he'd worry about her. There were going to be things brought out today that would hurt her more than the death of her brother-in-law. Not that she'd mourned his death overly much, especially if this morning was any gauge.

He'd woken slowly, his body easing into wakefulness much like he did most things in his life. But when he looked up at the woman riding him, he'd nearly came just from that sight alone. As he reached for her, she told him to be still.

"Let me have my pleasure first." He wanted to tell her that she was giving him more than she had to be receiving, but he stilled. Feeling his nails thicken and elongate, he knew that his beast was wanting to come out as well. It took him several seconds to realize that his wolf was telling him to behave, to let her have what she wanted. And not to take her like he normally would. Randy had had a thought that his wolf liked the human as much as he did her wolf.

"I feel him. Your beast. I feel him running along your skin." He couldn't answer her and was sure that she didn't require him to anyway. Throwing back her head, she rode him in a slow, steady pace that had him moaning with each of her strokes. "I was going to suck on you to bring you to wake, but I needed to feel you inside of me more. You're so hard right now. But I'm going to taste you later if we have time."

"You're killing me." Her grin made him think that was her plan, and he nearly reached for her again. "When you come, I'm going to join you. Come deep inside of you until you're overflowing with my cum. Then I'm going to roll you over on this bed and fuck you until neither of us can walk."

"I'd like that." Her fingers twisted at her nipples, and he felt his body tighten more. He looked at her then, in all her glory, and knew that he'd never forget this time with her. They may all blur together, he thought, over time, but this one time seeing her like this would keep him warm even in his grave.

Her gait was getting less rhythmic and more desperate feeling as she leaned forward over him. Her hands braced at his side as her nipples grazed his chest each time she moved back and forth with each rise and lowering of her hips. He felt her sheath tighten around him, milking him as she fucked him. Randy tried his best not to touch her, to give her what she wanted, but he had to hold her or turn her and pound her hard. As soon as his fingers dug into her hips, he heard her moan softly as she nuzzled deep into his neck. He both wanted to slow her more to enjoy her and to make her hurry so that he could plummet over the edge, joining her in what was sure to be spectacular.

Molly grazed her teeth over his shoulder, and his balls tightened to his body. As her tongue followed the same journey as her teeth, Randy knew that he was going to come the moment her teeth broke the skin. Holding her hips in a tighter grip, his cock thick with his release, he nearly lost it when he felt her juices roll down his balls to curl around him. Moaning again, he begged her to let him go.

"Take me." Her words had the effect he knew they would. Rolling her to her back, he pulled her arm to his mouth as she licked his throat. Pounding hard into her, his body crying out for release, he bit down into her flesh even as she bit him. Screaming out his name, he held her head to him as she suckled at his throat. Randy came, spewing his seed deep within her as he drank from her as well. But it wasn't enough, he'd needed more, and so did —

"You should come back to me now." Randy looked at Phil, not really seeing him as his head was so full of lust he wanted to go find Molly and make love to her all over again. "Randy, the judge has been announced. And as much as my mother loves you, if you don't give her her due, then she will be pissy with you."

As if he'd summoned her, Hope Campbell, along with Austin and three men he knew in passing, walked into the room. Every one stood up as she seemed to float into the room and stood in front of the long table that had been provided for the council. When she sat down, the rest of the room, including the men with her, sat as well. Her look did not bode well for him because he was pretty sure she knew where his mind had been only moments before. Randy tried to tell his cock to behave, but he was still thinking of Molly, and he was having a hard time stressing how much he needed to pay attention.

"We're here to have a trial and, if need be, disposal of one Shawn Charles, panther mate to Shelly Charles and father of Shawn Charles, deceased. He is being tried for the death of a human by the name of Mary Katherine Barker Ravenhall and others." Randy looked at Phil. *Others?*

Randy looked at Shawn and saw that the man seemed not to have a care in the world and that he was somewhat put out by what was going on around him. He didn't seem to be nervous at all. In fact, he looked as if he were bored with the whole process. When Randy looked back at Molly, he could see that she, too, was confused about his seemingly cavalier attitude and wondered about it. But he looked back at Hope...Mrs. Campbell...when she asked for anyone to speak on behalf of the dead. Molly stood up and moved to the front of the room. He'd asked her to wear a dress and was glad now that CJ had had one that fit her. Christ, she looked good enough to eat. And that thought brought on all sorts of images he wanted to do to her again. He was so fucked right now.

After being sworn in, Molly sat down and looked around the room before settling her eyes on Phil. He was going to question her first and, if need be, Randy would later. Unlike human court proceedings, theirs was a bit more relaxed about such rules as mates talking to mates at trials and the way things were so formal. If anyone got out of hand in a human courtroom, they were taken out. Here, someone would shift and tear their throats out. Or Hope would kill them. There were less problems in their court system by far.

"Can you tell us what happened on the morning of the nineteenth?" Molly nodded, then looked at him. He could see the panic in her eyes, and when Phil stepped in front of her, blocking him off, he wanted to get up and knock him on his ass. But Molly started talking and he realized what Phil had been doing. He was giving her room. Molly would break down with Randy, as she'd done at home. But Phil frightened her a little, and she'd do what he needed her to do.

"Mary and I were out walking the estate. She'd been telling me how happy she was that she'd found a lawyer she could trust. She said she'd filed for divorce and that he was going to make sure that she was...she said she trusted him."

"What did I tell her? What sort of deal did I make with your sister? Did she tell you?" He could hear the soft tone that Phil was using and wanted to tell him she would need more from him, but she spoke again.

"You told her that she would get what she wanted, a divorce. That Carter wouldn't be able to bully you into anything. She told me that you'd explained to her that

Carter would not know what you were doing until it was too late. Until they were well and truly divorced. And that you...she told me you told her that you weren't greedy like the other men she'd hired. That there would be no way that Carter could buy you off, even if he had enough money to do so. Which I guess he didn't. You're very wealthy in your own right."

"That's right. I don't have any need for money, especially ill-gained money like he would have tried to offer me. And did she tell you why?" Molly must have answered him in the affirmative because Phil went on. "I told her that Carter was a money grubbing bastard, and that proved to be correct, did it not?"

"He only stayed with her because she'd made it big. She said she was going to start over, that none of the money or the house had ever meant anything to her. She loved what she did and found it was more of something she enjoyed rather than a job." Randy looked at her when Phil finally moved. Molly looked at him. "I've found that...my sister would never have loved him. Not ever. She thought she could, but I know now that she never would have. I know now that I should have done something sooner to get her to leave him. He'd only married her because he'd blackmailed her into it. He thought he held something over her head."

"And what was that?" Phil hadn't moved in front of her again, but he did walk by her. Molly followed him with her eyes before looking back at Randy. He could feel her strength now. She would do this.

"He'd killed a woman while drunk, a child really. Carter had told Mary that he'd go to the police with the information that he'd made up and that they'd believe him over her. That my sister and I were nothing more than trash and he was so much better. He seemed to think he had a great deal more power in the town than he did. It wasn't until later that I found out what he'd done, and by then they were married. It was then that I tried to talk her into leaving him. She said she would when he put her into the hospital."

"You killed her, you know?" Everyone turned to Shawn, who spoke while laughing. "You're the reason that he had to resort to other means to make sure he wasn't left in the cold. The man was besotted with his wife, and everyone who worked at the house knew it. The only reason—" Hope cut Shawn off.

"When it's your turn, you can speak. But right now, no one is talking to you. Shut up or I'll shut you up. And you know damn well that if I do, it won't be with a gag. I'll remove your tongue." Shawn bowed before her, but his smile was sinister looking. Randy had a feeling that he was up to something. He just looked too confident that he wasn't going to be held accountable for his part in Mary's death.

The rest of Molly's part in telling the courts what sort of life that Mary had endured as Carter's wife was just as heart pulling. Randy found himself tense, and his wolf wanted to find Carter and kill him again. The fact that he'd died from a massive heart attack did little to make him feel like the man had gotten what he deserved. But he was dead and gone, buried in a small grave without as much as a marker to tell people where the bastard was. Then it was Shawn's turn to speak.

He took the seat near the long table and sneered at them all. Randy watched him closely in the event that he'd somehow gotten a gun or something in, but should have known better. He'd been pulled into a cell several days ago and had been strip searched. Then when the silver chain had been put around his throat, he'd been left naked and alone since then. His own mate would not have been able to see him, had she tried to visit the bastard.

"You are being accused of killing nine people. Seven of them human." Shawn looked at Hope as she named off the people. Randy had no idea that Carter and Shawn had been robbing people since they'd met all those years ago, long before he met the Barker women. But their life of crime together had been long and profitable for them both apparently.

"He needed help in his career, so he hired me to work for him. So…well, I did. And you can't try me for those crimes. I worked for him and as such, can't be held accountable for what a human might make me do for him. It was all his fault. As his slave, it was my duty to do as I was told." The room started mumbling when Hope stood up. Shawn laughed. "Oh, do sit down. You've no proof that I hurt anyone. And even if you had, you know the laws as well as I do that I had to do what he told me. Why, even my own mate will testify that I was working with him and that I'd only done what he'd told me every time I pulled the trigger."

Shawn looked around the room and frowned. Randy knew that he was looking for his mate, but it would do him no good. She'd gone to the council and asked for their bond to be dissolved. She'd told them that he wasn't her true mate but someone that could cook well and get him into the finest houses. She'd been granted it just after Jodie had been called in to read her mind.

"She's not here." Randy stood up just as Shawn stood to look around. "Your mate, she's not here. And she had written out a statement about how you worked for Carter

Ravenhall. And so you know, once you got paid by Carter to do those things, you were no longer his slave but his accomplice. You are just as guilty as he was. More so since you pulled the trigger."

"Not true. She would know better than to not do as I've told her to do. She knows who the master is in our household. I suppose it was too much for her to come here. Things like this are too much for women. Real women, anyway." He looked over at Molly, who waved. Randy didn't know what was going on, but he knew that she was in on it. Randy was going to enjoy this, he just knew it.

"Yes, well, real women, and I include your wife in this, are women who know when something is wrong and do something about it. And she did. But I think you'll be surprised by her statement, your mate's, I mean. She was under the impression that you not only were partners with Carter, but had suggested that he kill off his wife before the divorce were to go through. You can't imagine how terrified she was that you'd do the same to her. Anyway, I digress. She stated that you told Carter that he would be better off with some young wife he could control instead of one that listened to her sister." Randy handed him a copy of his wife's statement and watched as he read it over quickly. When he tossed it to the floor, Randy knew that he was nervous now.

"All lies. You made her sign this. She'd not turn in her mate. It's not allowed." Randy went to get the book that Tristian had given him. Molly had marked all the sections he'd need for today. In it was a section about testifying against your mate. "You can show that to me, but I know that it's for wolves only. I'm not a wolf in the event you didn't know that already, pup."

"Actually, it's not. A book for wolves. This one was written for all paranormal." He opened the book, careful of the pages. "This book was written long before I was born, and if I don't miss my guess, before you were born as well. It's a book of laws. Simply called *Abide by Them*." He looked at Shawn when he made a coughing noise. "I can see by your face you've heard of this book. But that's not all, is it? You know a great deal about it."

"It was lost. Long ago, someone said it had been destroyed." Randy showed him the book, again careful of it. He wasn't going to give anyone the chance to even touch a single page. "How do I know you didn't just make that up and now are going to spout laws that you've made up to suit yourself?"

"Give it to me." They all turned to Rob, mate to Hope, when he stood up. "I'm the historian to all supernaturals, and I can tell whether or not a book is a fake. If you'd be so kind as to trust me with it for just a moment, I'll tell everyone whether or not it's the real thing."

Randy looked at Tristian who actually owned the book. At his nod, he took it to Rob, and wasn't surprised to see him pull on a pair of white gloves before opening the book. It took Rob several minutes to scan some of the pages and the entire time, it stayed the book that he'd needed. Twice more it had changed its appearance since he'd had it, and he.... He decided he'd think about the images of him with seven children later. Right now he had to finish this so he could go home.

Randy watched Shawn as it was being tested. Gone was the confident man. Shawn was suddenly very nervous. He kept shifting on his seat and looking around the room as if he were looking for an escape route. When

Rob said he was finished with the book, he handed it back. He then looked around the room.

"The book is authentic. It was written by the first of us all. A vampire, a wolf, and a dragon. They used their own blood as ink to put the laws and rules here. And when they were done, they took it to each clan of other supernaturals and had them sign it. The blood of us all make this book real, its laws within are true." Rob turned to him. "You will allow me to read this when this is finished? I would so enjoy it. I promise to be very careful with it."

Randy looked at Tristian again and was happy to see that he agreed. Then he turned when he heard a low growl. The sight before him was so surreal that he nearly dropped the book. He did take a step back when Molly broke Shawn's neck. Hope fell to the floor on her knees as her breath returned to her body. Shawn had held the older vampire in his grip until that moment.

"He tried to kill me." Hope spoke while rubbing her bruised throat. A silver blade skittered across the floor as Molly kicked it from behind Hope. "I never saw him move. He was sitting there one moment, and the next...."

Everyone looked at Molly. She was holding a long blade now that had been handed to her by someone at the council. He was talking to her in low tones, but whatever he was saying, Molly didn't want to do. Randy started for her when Reid stepped in front of him.

"She has to finish him." Randy looked at his brother. "It's her right to end him. And she must. It's her duty to the council. And to Hope."

"Duty? What the fuck are you talking about?" When he tried to walk around him, Reid stopped him again. "Let me go to her."

"Randy, he tried to kill Hope. All Molly did was harm him when she broke his neck, and we both know it. If she doesn't end his life soon, then he'll be set free to stand trial again. This one for touching Hope. He'll go free after that. There is no death penalty for touching her." He looked at Molly, then at his brother, who nodded. Randy moved around him and went to Molly. She looked at him pleadingly, and he felt his heart ache for her.

"Kill him." She shook her head, and he leaned to her ear to speak to her. He could hear Shawn's heart starting to pump again and was fearful it might be too late. "He will go free if you don't. You've read the rules, love. You know as well as I do that he'll never see another cell so long as he lives. The trial here will be put on the backburner so that he can be put on trial for harming one of the council. But he'll be free then, and do you think anyone will ever see him again? He'll flee and never stand trial for your sister's death."

"But he's dead. I broke his neck." He told her to listen, and when she heard it, the faint heartbeat, he knew she would do it. "Stand back."

He moved to stand near Hope, who much to his amazement was sobbing. He would have sworn the woman didn't have any tear ducts, but she was proving him wrong. When he handed her his handkerchief, she took it and smiled at him. It hit him then—she was faking it. Good Christ, he had a moment to realize that she'd planned this whole thing.

"You old bat." She kissed his cheek and smiled again. "I'm going to tell your son you're a pushover. To think that you're doing this to get attention. And my poor Molly is going to be really pissed at you as well when she finds out."

"Then we'll just have to make sure that she never does. Won't we, dear boy? I'd hate to have to tell her about some of the things I know you did as a child." He shook his head as she continued. "I'm doing this so that she does what she needs to do." They both watched as the sword swung around, and just as it touched Shawn's neck, he opened his eyes. Randy stared him in the face as his head was removed from his shoulders.

Molly stood there looking at Shawn's body as it slumped forward. Randy moved two steps toward her when she looked at him. The look in her eyes told him two things. She was terrified and was relieved at the same time. He took the last two steps toward her just as Hope moved behind her table again.

"She was coming to me." He looked at Molly as Hope spoke to the room in general. He was holding her as she stood stiffly, still holding the sword. "Mrs. Campbell was coming to me because I had the names of the people who had signed the book. Two of them are still alive and here today. I thought she'd need them. One of them is a panther like Shawn is...was."

Randy looked around not really caring about the book at the moment. He held onto Molly as she started back to her seat. He was stopped when one of the bailiffs said Molly's name. "The mistress would like to speak to you. If you'd be so kind as to follow me, my lady, she will meet you in one of the offices just here."

"I need to help her to her chair first." The man shook his head, and that's when he realized he was talking about Molly. "I don't think now is a good time. She's just been...I think she needs to have a seat."

"I would like to thank you on behalf of all the council." He and Molly both turned to the table as Hope spoke again. "Today you saved my life. And as such, we have agreed to grant you a gift. One that we rarely bestow on anyone as young as you."

"No thanks." Molly sat down and stood up again when Hope quirked a brow at her. "I'm sorry, but you'll have to forgive me. I don't want any more gifts. I think I've had enough given to me for a while now. In fact, if I could figure out how to get rid of a few that I have now, I'd gladly give them up. So whatever you think I deserve, please just...why don't you give it to Austin? I have a feeling he could use a little help."

Several people laughed and Hope moved around the table. This time she was followed by the other members of the council, including Austin. Randy didn't like the look in his face. It said something he was going to learn from was going to come his way and with it a little pain. He'd given him that look when he'd been a young pup.

"You really don't have a choice. And as such, you're going to have to take it." Molly took a step back when Hope put out her hand. "I'm sorry, love, but it will only hurt for a moment."

The pain was incredible. And it surged through his body as if Hope had touched him. He tried to hang onto consciousness but felt it slipping away. The sound of the dropping sword had him looking to Molly just as she was caught up by Reid. He thought he might get mad at him later about it, but right now he was pitching forward too. The blackness took him, and he could have sworn he heard Austin laughing.

CHAPTER 12

The entire pack was there. Nancy knew that they'd have a good turnout this full moon and had had extra people helping out with food. Tonight her son gave up half his pack, and she thought that the two groups were going to be better for it. She looked up when CJ said her name.

"She's throwing up again." Nancy had to hide her smile. Poor Molly. She wasn't dealing well with all the attention. "I tried to tell her it wasn't that bad, but she won't hear of it. I think she's going to be too weak to shift if she does it much more. Who knew a person could throw up so much without eating a damned thing?"

"She'll be fine." Nancy tightened her fist again and tried her best to ignore the pain in her chest. She knew that she was dying. But she was pretty sure she'd hidden it well enough all these weeks. But now...she was sure that there would be no more hiding it after tonight. The only person who had suspected a thing was Reid, and she'd convinced him that she was going to be fine. She knew for sure that she was far from it.

The food started from the pack kitchen to make its way to the tables that had been set up. Nancy worried for a few minutes whether or not they had enough tables, but then one of the other women, Sarah she thought her name was, started directing the younger pups into setting up more. Nancy thought she might work well with Molly when this was done. She looked at CJ and Alexis as they moved along the tables putting spoons and serving forks into some of the dishes. It was going to be a good meal.

"Is that Sarah Westinghouse?" They both looked to where she'd pointed. CJ nodded. "I thought so. You should have her go and help Molly. She's going to need a full-blood to help her with her daily activities after tonight. Perhaps she can even help her with the set-up of their meetings, too. She'll need someone of her own to ease her into being a good alpha person."

"I was thinking the same thing." She loved CJ with all her heart and started to tell her that when another pain gripped her. The small moan had both women coming toward her.

"I'm fine. Just a little tired." Neither one looked as if they believed her, and she wanted to kiss them both. But she had to distract them somehow. "Did I tell you that there will be a new shop opening in town? It's supposed to cater to small children. A bookstore that will need a boost if she's to make a go of it. I understand from her that she's going to pledge to Phil tonight. Her mate was killed some time ago and she's raising her young child on her own."

"I met her the other day. She's half vampire like Phil and had the abilities to be a day walker. They talked a great deal about what she'd have to do." Holly sat beside her and touched her forehead as she continued speaking. "You okay, Mom? You look a little pale. You're not doing too much, are you?"

"I most certainly am not." But she had been, and they all knew it. When she stood up, she pretended to be engrossed in a bowl of green beans as the pain subsided. She just needed to get through tonight and she could go to bed and rest. She knew it was close but needed to make sure all her children were safe first. Her mate, he'd come for her twice now.

"I've got to make sure they will be well loved." He'd clicked his tongue at her, something he'd done when he'd been alive. *"They will need each other when I go."*

"They have each other. You just wish to make me wait as you've always done. Do you ever get ready when you say you will?" He'd moved so close to her that night that she would swear she could feel his breath. *"I've missed you, love. Come to me."*

"Soon." She'd watched him fade away with a promise that he'd be back. It was going to be tonight. And they both knew it.

Nancy moved toward her sons, needing them in a way she'd never thought she would before...all them, including the ones that she'd fallen for when they were brought to her to heal. Myles kissed her cheek as she hugged him to her. This man had done so much that she would miss him a great deal. Next, she hugged Connor to her. Her baby.

"I've a good mind to beat your bottom again." He looked at her, shocked, and she just knew that he was trying to think what she'd found out. Nancy laughed. "You're a good boy. And you'll be fine. I was just thinking how many times you'd get me distracted with one tale or another as a child and I'd forget what I was about. You were very good at that."

"I still am. I don't always get around it with Lou. I think she is more focused than you were at times. But I will be great. Lou keeps me in line well enough. And our children make me glad that I found her." Nancy patted his cheek and looked at Phil. He was looking at her as if he knew and she was pretty sure he did. Nothing escaped the man's notice she'd come to realize.

"You'll be fine then? It's not too late, you know. I can still give you what you denied me all these years." She shook her head at his question as he pulled her to him for a hug. "I've lost a good many friends over the centuries. But I shall miss you most of all, I think. You're like a second mother to me."

Her heart swelled with love, and she couldn't talk. Nodding once at him, she was let go from the hug, but he held her. They'd talked long ago about her living well past her time to be with them just a bit longer. Phil had kept his word all these years and had not given her the life-giving magic that he had the rest of the family. Phil would hold them together and would be the best person for this family in the coming weeks.

Dallas was next.

"Did you know that Stacey told me that you were expecting again?" He grinned at her, and she wanted to stay to see the child that would be born to them. But she had to go. If she stayed for this birth, she'd stay for another and another until it was too long. She wanted to rest. Her mate needed her as much as she did him. She really was very tired.

"We found out today that it's twins. Boys, they said. They didn't tell us if they're identical yet, but I'm betting they are. Stacey said she thinks so, too." Twin boys like hers. She nodded at him and hugged him. She would miss him so much. "Stacey is hoping you'll come stay with us when they come. She seems to think that I'm going to be spoiling them rotten as I did the others. I don't think so."

"You'll spoil them no matter if I'm there or not. But as for staying, we'll see." She moved to her other son and knew a great and profound love. Gordon was her favorite, though if anyone asked, she'd tell them they were insane. She knew it was because he reminded her so much of her own love. Not in looks so much but in temperament. He was truly his father's son.

"You've outdone yourself again." Gordon kissed her forehead as he held her to him. "I think you enjoy this as much as you do watching the children. They both bring you such joy. I'm thinking we need to start hiring you out to other packs so they can get as organized as you always seem to be. We'll be rich beyond our wildest dreams."

Tears clouded her vision as another pain took her breath. She was glad now that Gordon held her, and when he looked down at her with a frown, she waved him off. Let him think it was happiness when the pain was taking her away from them all.

After talking with her children for a bit longer, she made her way back to the women. Each of them were seated in chairs of honor being waited on by the younger pups. These women were all like her own children. Sitting down, she reached for Molly's hand and held it. She only hoped that she'd forgive her someday. This girl, so new to the family, was going to be the strength that held them together when things were at their worst. The girl had no idea what her talent was going to do for them all. Not even her.

"I'd like to tell you something. Each of you." Holly looked concerned, but Nancy waved her off much like she had her son. "I'm going to be fine. Just fine. But I would like to do something I've been thinking about doing for a long time. And tonight is the night. It's the passing of the spoon."

"Oh for heaven's sake. We all know you have more than one of those things. Are you giving us each one?" CJ laughed, as did the rest of them. Nancy did as well and shook her head when they calmed.

"I've a stash of them, yes, but I'm talking about the one that my mother gave to me when I met my mate. She said that it would come to mean a great deal to everyone as it had to her. She said that the wooden spoon that she gave me would be passed from her generation to mine and so on. She had been the fourth one to receive it in a long line of wolf women. And as the fifth one, I need to pass it on now that all of my children are happy."

Nancy pulled the spoon from her pocket and held it out. Even after all these years the spoon still looked new. It was nothing like the one she used on their stubborn heads most of the time, but it was close. She ran her fingers over the smoothed out surface from many hands using it as her own mother had done when she'd been handing it to her. She supposed it was the magic that held it as so. She looked at the women around her and smiled.

"When I was given this spoon, I was told that it would keep my children in line, bring new blood to the family, and would forever be the one thing that all would remember. I never really understood that until you ladies came into my life." She looked at Holly. "Even you, my dear. You've all seen me use it on the boys. I've even used it on you once or twice, but you've never seen it being used for what it's for. The spoon holds magic that heals like nothing else can. It's filled with magic that only the person who receives it can use."

"You use it to make the broth that you've given each of us when we've been ill." She turned to Molly, knowing that she'd be the one to understand. "The day I was in the clinic, when I'd first come here. Someone told me that you'd made the broth and that you made it so special that everyone got better because of it. The spoon is what you stirred it with and it made me better quicker. Is that what you mean?"

"It is." She rubbed her fingers over the smooth wood and pulled it to her heart as another pain held her. She looked down at the spoon, knowing that it was working its magic even now, giving her the time that she needed to do this. It was taking away some of the pain so that they'd not notice what was going on. "I've come to a decision, and I know who would carry it along to hand to the next generation. I hope that—"

"Molly." They all looked at CJ when she spoke. "It's her, isn't it? She'll be the one to keep us in line after you're gone. I, for one, think it's a wonderful idea."

Nancy looked around the circle and could see the others nodding their heads. Molly was the only one who was shaking her head. The girl could be too stubborn.

"You should give it to your daughter. I don't think I'm the one who should have it." The others started to talk, but Holly stood up and knelt before Molly. "I don't want to take your heritage. I'm nothing more than an addition to this family, you've all been here...all of you have so much more to give than I do. Holly should have it."

"Take my heritage? Oh, Molly love, we're all family here. You're taking nothing from me, but preserving what the rest of us will need in the future." Holly looked at her and Nancy knew her daughter was aware of what she was doing and why. Giving her the spoon was her last deed on this earth, and Holly was helping her make it right. "My mother has been holding it for you and only you. Haven't you, Mom?"

"I have." Nancy handed her the spoon and with trembling fingers she took it. The magic passed from her to Molly in a small curl of white magic, and she felt it immediately. She'd done the right thing, and the person who would use it as she'd done would know just what to do. And maybe she'd hit a few empty heads while she was at it. Nancy watched the woman tease poor Molly about her lack of cooking skills and smiled at her face. She'd learn to cook, Nancy knew, if it was the last thing she did.

Standing up when the meeting was called to order, Nancy slipped into the house to find a place to rest. She found Tristian there, waiting for her it seemed. The man had dressed up for the meeting, it appeared to her, but when he nodded toward her and bowed, she knew that he'd done it for her.

"I would be honored to help you to your room." She didn't ask him what he meant. She was suddenly too weak to play any more games. "Shall I carry you?"

"Not if you don't want me to hurt you." He laughed and she did as well. They moved to the staircase and stood looking at it. So many memories here, and now she was going to leave them all behind.

"No, you shan't." She looked at him. "As much as I'd like to say I read your mind, I didn't. You spoke aloud. All the memories you have of your family will follow you on your road. Some of them will bring a mist to your eyes, but there will be enough good ones that you'll never want for things to make you smile. You have loved well and hard, my lady, and I envy you in this. I shall miss you greatly."

"I'll miss them." They started up the stairs. "All of them and even you, you old buzzard. I'll miss you too."

She was nearly halfway up when another pain hit her, this one so powerful that she was sure she was going to die on the stairs instead of the bedroom she'd come to love. She'd made it her own special place, a place she could die like she had lived, with her family around her. Nancy needed to be there when she passed. However would her beloved find her?

Tristian picked her up into his arms, and she had no strength to protest. It wasn't just when she was going to die tonight, it was how quickly. He put her on her bed a few seconds later, and she felt her body begin its process of closing down. She looked up at him when he kissed her forehead softly.

"You've everything you need, love?" She nodded at him and watched as he moved to the door. She stopped him with a word.

"You'll watch over them for me?" He nodded, and she could see his tears, and her heart hurt for this man as much as it did for her children. "You can't say you'll miss me again. You'll have me blubbering like an old woman."

"I shall not say it then. But you'll know the truth of my words." He moved back to the bed and took her hand into his and kissed it. "You are the greatest woman I've ever met. You're leaving a legacy behind that all will envy. Your name will be said with reverence and love. Your children's children's children will talk about you as if they had known you. And in a way, I suppose they will. You can die in peace, my lady. For you have done so much."

She laid back on the silken pillow that had been hers and her mate's on their wedding night and closed her eyes. A small sound had her opening them again, and there he stood. Her love, her mate. The one who had died so young but had given her the world.

"You're ready for me then?" She smiled at him and stood up. Nancy was amazed at how good she felt and wondered if the vampire had given her his blood. "Nay, 'tis your new life that gives you this. See? You are mine now and have moved from this world to the next. I have missed you."

Turning, she saw her body at rest. Breath no longer moved her chest up and down, and she knew that she had died peacefully. Looking back at her true love, she held him in her arms as she thought they moved from this world to another. But when they started away, she felt the tug of the spoon. Moving toward it, she knew what they were to do.

"Aye, we're her magic." They stood in front of Molly as she held the spoon to her heart. The others stood nearby, and Nancy knew that she'd be able to watch over them and help this girl do so. All at once, they were sliding into it and being greeted by all their families. It was them, all of them that had helped her all these years as she would her own children. Nancy felt at peace and knew that everything would be fine now.

~~~

CJ found Austin in his mother's room again. Since the funeral two days ago, he'd been in there more often than not. The man was dying inside and all of them could see it. CJ moved into the room and sat on his lap. He held her, but she knew that he wasn't really seeing her. He had been so close to his mother that he was hurting more than any of them were.

"I found her photo album today. It was as if she'd put it out for me to see. I looked over her old pictures and saw you and your brothers in a lot of the past faces." He nodded but stared at the bed. They would never take this room apart but leave it as she'd left it. "Did you know that your dad had a brother?"

"Yes. He died when he was small. I don't know from what, but I wasn't born yet. Mom said he'd been young, but he'd never shifted." He shifted under her weight and tried to set her away from him, but she wouldn't let him. "I'll be down for dinner soon. I just want to sit here for a little while longer."

"Dinner was nine hours ago, Austin. We're now on our way to breakfast. And the children want to know if you'll come hug them goodbye as they head off to school. Or will you ignore their grief for your own?" He looked at her, and she knew he was trying to gauge if she was kidding or not. But he finally nodded his head and they both stood up. As he left the room with her, he turned back once more to look at it.

"I'd never been in here when she was alive. I had no idea she'd done this to it." The room was covered in framed photographs. They covered every flat surface too. Some of them were old, and a good many of them were new. There was even one of Randy and Molly when they'd been over for dinner the week before the pack meeting. She'd kept them with her even in her death. He was glad now that she'd come up to rest and had left them peacefully in here and not on the ground somewhere.

"She loved to take pictures. And she'd get frames from us every time we went into town. I think I would pick up more frames for her than I would groceries for us in any given week." Austin nodded as they made their way to the stairs. "Some of those pictures are in the album I found. I think she had prints made of the ones she loved."

"She did. Mom had me take a bunch of them to the print shop to be reprinted. I'd had most of them framed for her while I was there thinking it would be a nice treat for her. She fussed at me for two days. Said that some pictures had to pick their frames, not have some man shoving them in a wooden box like they needed to be there. I had to take them all apart for her and vowed never to do that again. I can see now that she was right. Some of the pictures I had had framed look so much better in the ones she put them in." He laughed a little, something she'd not heard him do for a while. "I miss her so much."

She started to tell him they all did, but they were moving into the kitchen then. She'd been surprised when his brothers had shown up an hour ago, and since she'd been gone getting Austin, more family had shown up. They filled the kitchen like they did most spaces, with loud voices and a deep love for each other. There were even a few arguments about what to have for a snack, which usually meant an entire meal.

"Ah, there you are. We thought you'd never get down here." Gordon handed him his daughter and a spoon with some liquid in it. "Taste this. Molly swears she followed the recipe to the letter, but I think she left something out. Like flavor. It sort of tastes like water with salt in it."

"You know I'm standing right here." Molly slapped Gordon and took the spoon from Austin. "I told them I couldn't cook. And they insisted that I could because I'd been given the spoon. And it has flavor. I put about a cup of that spice in it I saw on the counter." She laughed with them all, and Austin declared it unfit. Which she supposed was what Molly had been working toward. If you couldn't cook, then no one would ask you to.

Molly hit Austin in the head and grinned at him. Austin looked like he was going to hit her. Then his face broke into a smile. "She gave it to you then? I suppose you think you'll be able to get away with it as much as she did. But it doesn't work that way. She was my mom, and you are my sister. Big difference."

"I do, as a matter of fact, and why shouldn't I? When she handed it to me, she said I was being given the power of protection and that no one was to harm me or face the squad of children." Austin looked at her before looking at Molly again.

"Squad of children?" About that time, the door flew open and Austin was brought down by the squad. The children from the entire family tackled him to the floor, kissing and hugging every part of him that they could get to. When he started laughing, the children doubled their efforts until parents started to pull them off him. Austin laid there for several seconds before he spoke to her. He held onto her leg when she started to move out of his reach.

"This was your idea, I suppose?" She shook her head at him and watched as two of the men pulled him up. "You didn't have anything to do with this?"

"Oh, I didn't say that. I said I didn't come up with the idea." They looked at Phil when he cleared his throat. "He did it."

"I had to get you down here. I have to talk to you all." CJ didn't like the look on his face and nearly told him some other time. But he shook his head. "It's time. I have to read the will. Once we get the children off to school. It's important that we do this, not just for us but for Nancy as well. She would be pissed if she knew that we'd put if off because we were hurting."

An hour later they were seated around the large dining room table and CJ wanted again to tell Phil no. They had sobered up after he'd told them why he'd done this and now it was time. She looked at Austin when he reached for her hand. She could feel his pain like it was her own. And she supposed it was. They had both loved her so much. Looking around the room, she could see that the rest of them were holding hands as well. This might be harder on them than her funeral had been or finding her that morning.

She'd found her. CJ had called up to her room twice and when she didn't answer, she went up to see if she was going into town with her. They'd been planning this trip to the mall for a few days, and Molly was going to meet them after her interview. CJ stared at her for several minutes, knowing that she had to check on her but knew the moment she'd opened the door that she was gone. It was the smile on her face, the serene smile that had her believing that Nancy had simply slipped away in her sleep and had not suffered at all. CJ looked down the hall when she heard Austin coming toward her.

He'd stopped moving when he saw her. CJ was sure he saw she was crying, and he dropped to his knees. Tears fell down his cheeks unchecked as he kept telling her no. Over and over he cried out until CJ finally went to him. Helping him up, he staggered with her to Nancy's room to see his mother. They both held her hands while they waited for Reid. She was glad now that he'd been the one to come to them and not some stranger. Reid had made sure that she was taken away and things were set into motion to have her buried. Austin had talked to him after the funeral and CJ still had no idea what he'd said to the young man.

"This is the last will and testament of Nancy Gordon Force, wife of Austin Dallas Force, deceased." Phil looked at them all and CJ realized that this was going to make things final, more so than her being put into the ground had done. "It's not as bad as you think. She was a very wealthy woman after her mate died and never touched it in all her years. But she did with it what she thought best. It's what I would have done; it's what I think she had planned even before she called me to help her."

He handed them each an envelope, and CJ noticed that even Molly got one. As they held them, Phil went on to explain that all her money was to be divided up among the grandchildren, and each of them were to use it to start something. She had anticipated that there would be in the neighborhood of about seventy, Phil said with a straight face. She'd provided for them in ways she thought would make them remember her.

"Nancy thought if they ever wanted to have their own business, then it would be their start money. Seed money, she called it." CJ nodded. She'd heard her call her cookie jar money just that. "And the things she wanted especially for you, she put there in those envelopes. I don't know what is in them, for those were sealed when she handed them to me. She handed me Molly's just before the pack meeting. Each of you are to keep what is there to your heart, where she said it would do you the most good. The old bat even gave me one. I found it in the envelope when I opened it yesterday."

No one opened their envelope. Tears were flowing freely now as some of them looked at their treasure and some even held it to their hearts. CJ knew that she'd wait to read hers, coming to grips with this way hard enough. She'd loved that woman almost as much as she did her own grandmother. She traced each letter of her name with her finger and thought of the wonderful woman who had written it for her. Her name across the seal made her heart ache a little more.

"I'd like to propose a toast." Everyone stood up when Austin did. He held his glass high, and CJ thought it appropriate that it was just a glass of water. Nancy would have loved it. "To the greatest woman ever to touch our lives. May each of us remember her all our days and the sage though sometimes strange advice that she gave us. To my mother, to the mother of all of us in one way or another. Mom, we will always miss you."

Each of them agreed and drank down what they had. CJ looked around the room and realized at that moment that these people were her family. And nothing in the world would tear them apart.

EPILOGUE

Randy sat in his chair and held his opened envelope in one hand and his drink in the other. He had no idea what to do about either. He heard his brother coming down the hall and had to smile. He knew that he'd come over sooner or later. Randy was sure his letter said basically the same thing. Randy sat up when he came into his office.

"Did you open yours?" Reid poured himself a drink at the bar before sitting down across from him. Randy nodded. "Do you believe this shit? What the hell was she thinking? We're grown men and now she springs this on us? I ask again, what the hell was she thinking?"

"That she loved us?" Reid didn't say anything as he watched the fire crack and pop in the grate. Randy wasn't sure what Nancy had been thinking either, but he loved her for it. "I called Phil. I asked him when this was done. He said two weeks after we came here."

Reid looked at him and smiled. "That might explain a bit. I called him too. He was pissy about me calling him. Said I should come here and talk to you. We had a lot to discuss. He said...did you know she'd done this? I mean, did Phil ever tell you anything about what she'd done?"

Randy shook his head. He'd had no clue. Looking at the adoption papers again, he nearly wept when he saw that he'd been Randal James Force since he'd been seventeen years old. And had he known, he would have called himself that. He started to say something to Reid when he spoke first.

"I don't know if I would have changed my name or not. I mean, I might have back then but thinking now, I don't know." Randy waited for him to explain. His brother smiled before he continued. "I would have loved to have been called that as a kid, I mean, who wouldn't? But now.... Now, knowing that she'd done this for us without any fanfare makes it all the more special. Like she'd given us a great gift to have forever. Am I making any sense?"

Randy liked that idea. Forever. She'd given them something they'd have as their own. Something as physical as a hug. She told them that she loved them as a son. And more than that, she'd given them something no one could ever take from them.

When Reid left just before sunrise, Randy heard Molly coming down the stairs. She had her interview this morning, and he wondered why she was nervous. As soon as she appeared around the corner to his new office, she smiled at him and leaned against the doorjamb.

"I can smell Reid. When did he get here?" He told her just before midnight. "I guess you and he were talking about what Nancy gave you. Is he all stuffy about it? Or did he take it like a man?"

"We were. And yeah, you know Reid. He's the really stuffy sort. She adopted him as well, I guess you know." Molly nodded and moved into the room and sat on his lap. He'd long since taken off his shirt and sat there now in only his pants and socks. "You have entirely too many clothes on."

She had on a tee-shirt and maybe a pair of panties. He reached under her shirt when she shifted over his lap so that she was facing him, and he cupped her full breast. Her moan had him leaning forward and suckling on her nipple through her shirt.

"I've been thinking you need to relax me some. I'm very nervous." He nipped at her breast before sliding his hand up her thigh to her hip and discovered she was pantie-less as well. "I told you I was thinking about this. Will you help me? I want to make a good impression today."

"I love the way you think." Picking her up, he sat her on the desk and spread her legs. "You're already wet, too. I think I'd like to have my breakfast now. And in the meantime if you're relaxed when I've had my fill, then all the better."

He didn't wait for her to answer but buried his face between her legs. She lifted her hips to his mouth when he toyed his tongue around her clit. Opening her wider with his fingers, Randy suckled her clit into his mouth as he slid his fingers deep into her pussy. She tasted better every time he did this and decided that he'd die a happy man if she would allow him this every morning until the end of their days.

She tasted of the sweetest wine and the most addictive drugs. He drank from her, losing himself in her as he filled himself with her juices. Every time she would raise her hips up, he'd slow his exploration of her and wait for her to settle again. His cock began to hurt when she curled her fingers into his hair. Her breaths were coming in short pants, and he had to adjust his cock or hurt himself more.

"Finish me." He smiled around her but didn't stop teasing her. He loved drinking from her and wanted more and more of it. When she lifted his head, he could see that she was hurting. Freeing his cock, he stood up and moved between her legs.

His cock fit her. It was all he could think about as he moved slowly into her. She wrapped around him like a sheath, and he never wanted to leave her. As he moved in and out of her, taking his time, she laid back on the desk and tore her shirt from her body. Randy watched as she cupped her breasts and rolled her nipples between her finger and thumb. He loved that she took her pleasure when and how she wanted it. He loved her.

"You look so delicious laying here all spread out for me." She moaned and wrapped her ankles around his hips to bring him closer. Leaning over her, he braced his hands on either side of her and took her mouth. She moaned as she licked her cream off his mouth. When she pulled him over her, he felt her hard nipples brush against his chest, and he moaned with her.

"I want to mark you." He looked down at her, his balls so full and achy he nearly released when she spoke. "I need to make you mine. Will you let me, Randy? Will you let me bite you and leave a scar so that everyone can see it and know that you're all mine?"

He looked at her and fell in love with her more as she looked up at him. She was waiting for him to answer her but his throat was full of emotion and he wasn't sure he could talk around it. When he nodded, he pulled her body to his and stood up. She wrapped her arms around him as he moved to the wall, her ankles already locked at his hips.

He wanted her hard and fast, and this was closer than the bed upstairs. As soon as her back touched the wall, he started pounding into her hard with quick punches. Her tongue licked along his throat, and he knew she was waiting for him to say something. Tilting his head for her, he cried out when she sank her teeth deep into his neck. His cock exploded, and her body tightened around him as she joined him. Their climaxes screamed from their bodies. As he bit into her shoulder, he tasted her and realized that she was in heat.

Smiling, he felt his cock fill again and he took her to the floor. This time he was going to fill her with a child if she let him. Randy could think of nothing better than to see her swollen with their child.

"I want a child with you." She nodded. "I mean now. You're ready. If you say yes, we'll create a child tonight. And I'm betting it will be a daughter, just like you."

"Nancy." He nodded. The name was perfect. "Fill me, Randy. I want to have your baby. I need her, we all do."

Randy made love to his mate and knew that first thing in the morning...or at least later today...he was going to marry her. He wanted his wife to have his child, and he knew that Nancy Force would approve.

~~~

The Force men and women went on to have generation after generation of children. The packs grew until it was time to split them again, Austin to his son and Randy to his daughter. The pack became one that others would model their own by, adults would compare their own leadership by, as well as legends would be written about. And through it all, the spoon was passed from female to female, keeping them all in line and in good health.

"Do you believe anyone knows what we've done for them?" The first woman looked around at the magic that gave it what it was. "Do you think they believe in us?"

Nancy Force moved forward, a woman that had been with them the least amount of time but had taught them all so much. She smiled at her, and Daisy smiled back. But she didn't let the smile fool her. She'd never known a woman who could say so much with just a look.

"I think they know just who we are. Can you not feel their love whenever anyone uses our magic?" Daisy nodded and thought of how much stronger they were all because of it. "I daresay that in the years to come they will use the magic to do more than any of us ever dreamed of doing when we were there. Can you imagine watching what they'll do with it?"

Daisy nodded. But she really couldn't. In all the time she'd been here she'd seen so many changes herself that sometimes she had to take a deep breath. And now so much more was being said and done. Plus, there were the children. That had been the most pleasant surprise.

"It's taken us to them." Nancy nodded, and Daisy knew she was still basking in her newest grandchildren. Molly and Randy had had triplets, and each of them as beautiful as the next. But her heart was held by the oldest girl...Nancy, they'd called her.

When the children were born, Nancy had wanted to touch the children. Daisy had been standing next to her and had been pulled from their place to stand over the sleeping babe. When she opened her eyes, she didn't cry but stared at the two of them as if she could see them. It was then that Daisy had realized that she could. They'd been seeing the other children as well.

"When they shift, they can no longer see us, but they know we are there." Daisy nodded at her own mate. Randall had been with her twice today to see the others. She was sure it was what was making them all nearly fly with happiness.

Nancy had said that they needed not just to look at the children but to teach them. At first Daisy had wondered what they had to teach children of this day and age, but Nancy had pointed out that they needed to know about them. Daisy had been asking the others to write out some of their history so that all of them could teach the children. It was working out beautifully, too. Daisy watched as Nancy was pulled away. One of the children must need her. Daisy moved to the portal that had previously only been used to send out magic and moved through it. Her descendant was sitting in the corner with tears on his face.

"What are you doing here when you should be out playing with the others?" He glared at her but smiled when he saw it was her. "Have you pulled your sister's hair again?"

"No. I was bad at school. They told us to tell about our family, and I told them about you. She said I was making things up. Mom said I needed to learn to curb my tongue. I didn't know what that meant, and she punished me for it."

"That doesn't sound like your mom. Tell me what really happened." She knew that Chris, his mother, was a good mom and if he told her he was seeing them, she'd be more inclined to encourage him rather than sit him in a corner. He looked at her again and sobbed.

"I was mean to her. My mom, I was mean to her when she said that I would have to tell Mrs. James I was sorry. I'm not sorry, and I told Mommy she was a poo head." He cried more, and Daisy found herself hiding her laughter. This boy was so much like her own mate that it was not hard to tell that they were related. "I don't want her to be mad at me, but I'm not sorry I told Mrs. James she was wrong."

"I told you that she was wrong, too. But I also told you that you had to be nicer about saying so. You can't just tell people that they're liars when they don't agree with you." Daisy looked at Chris, who was swollen with another child. "Ben, didn't we have this talk about your speaking to your relatives? What did I tell you?"

"You said that I was lucky to be able to talk to them and that if others didn't believe me it was their problem. But she was so mean about it. Why did she make me feel like I was stupid?" Chris picked up her son and held him as he cried.

"Your uncle Austin has had a talk with her. And as much as I hate to agree with him because the man already has a big head, he fired her." Daisy looked at the boy who was smiling. "This does not justify you being mean to either of us, but she was wrong in making you tell the class you were retarded. I will not tolerate that, and neither will Austin."

After he left to go outside, Chris sat there for a little while. When she spoke, Daisy felt her heart fill with admiration and love for this woman.

"You do know that the other children are jealous, don't you?" Daisy looked around and realized that while she couldn't see her, Chris was speaking to her. "Not because of the gift you've given him, all of them, but because you side with his parents. They think it is so cool that you never let him get by with things. I think in a way, Ben does too. I wanted to...I want to thank you for that."

Daisy wanted to speak to her but was afraid to be disappointed. Instead she got up and made her way to her and touched her face gently. She knew that Chris felt her because she put her hand on the area.

"Thank you." Tears were rolling down her face, and Daisy had to wipe several times at her own. "We were talking…the others and me, the women of this pack, and we were wondering if you could tell Nancy how much we miss her. And, of course, how much we love her."

Daisy touched her again, and Chris nodded, then stood up as she made her way to the doorway and out of the room. She turned back and smiled. The look on her face reminded her so much of the love she'd had for her own children, and she felt her heart swell with a newfound love for this woman.

"I just thought of something else. It's no biggy if you don't want to do it. But I was wondering if you'd be the angel that watches over this child like you do Ben? Or even Nancy, but Ben loves you so much that it would mean a great deal to him and me if you could." She left the room, and Daisy sat there for a long time just thinking about another baby to see. When she left the house for her world, she found Nancy and told her everything.

"Well, of course, you'll watch over her. Why would you think you wouldn't? Those girls of mine are the best, and my sons? Well, there is none better than them either. They're a force of nature when it comes to love and family."

Daisy believed they were and felt proud of the fact that she was a part of their lives as well.

About the Author

Kathi Barton, author of the bestselling series Force of Nature, lives in Nashport, Ohio with her husband Paul. In addition to writing full time Kathi likes to spend time with her eight grandkids, three children and three children-in-laws. She writes to relax and have fun.

Her muse, a cross between Jimmy Stewart and Hugh Jackman brings them to life for her readers in a way that has them coming back time and again for more. Her favorite genre is paranormal romance with a great deal of spice. You can visit Kathi on line and drop her an email if you'd like. She loves hearing from her fans. aaronskiss@gmail.com.

Follow Kathi on her blog:
http://kathisbartonauthor.blogspot.com/

www.ingramcontent.com/pod-product-compliance
Lightning Source LLC
Chambersburg PA
CBHW022105170626
46808CB00002B/611